Southern Hospitality

SOUTHERN HOSPITALITY

Can an African American family from New Jersey find happiness and peace in the South?

DON KEEFER

iUniverse

SOUTHERN HOSPITALITY
CAN AN AFRICAN AMERICAN FAMILY FROM NEW JERSEY FIND HAPPINESS AND PEACE IN THE SOUTH?

iUniverse books may be ordered through booksellers or by contacting:

iUniverse
1663 Liberty Drive
Bloomington, IN 47403
www.iuniverse.com
1-800-Authors (1-800-288-4677)

ISBN: 978-1-4917-4529-8 (sc)
ISBN: 978-1-4917-4530-4 (e)

Library of Congress Control Number: 2014915196

Printed in the United States of America.

iUniverse rev. date: 10/06/2014

Contents

CHAPTER 1

Roger awakened to the sound of voices. He looked at the large clock over the doorway of the hospital room. It was a few minutes after midnight, and Deputy Kearns and Deputy Hazelit were debating why Kearns was several minutes late in relieving Hazelit. It ended with Hazelit telling Kearns, "Jes wait until the next time you all are waiting on me, jes wait." With that he put on his coat and stormed out of the room. Kearns looked over at Roger and said, "How you doin boy?"

Roger responded, "Fine until you and your friend woke me up. While you are here, please pour me a glass of water."

Kearns poured the water and said, "Jamie and those boys in the holding cell really did a job on you. You musta really pissed them off."

Roger grunted and said, "Yes, I guess I did. I fired Jamie at the plant a couple of months ago and he threatened that he would get even." While he was sipping the water, Roger asked, "Why do you hate blacks so much?"

Kearns looked puzzled for a moment and he responded, "I don't, it's just that they have their place and we whites have ours, which is the way the good Lord made things. The Klan is still around, but not like it was twenty, thirty years ago. Why over in Henderson County, they're even doing a food drive for poor whites and blacks for Christmas. I remember when I was a boy, two of my uncles were in the Klan and they were always trying to get my Dad to join, but he always said no. You see it's like a system, we stay on our side of the line, and the blacks stay on their side, and we all get along fine. Things go bad when someone don't know which side of the line they belong on.

Roger contemplated this for a few moments and said, "I was just wondering have you ever thought about what your life would be like if you were on the opposite side of that line?"

Kearns responded at once, "No, cause that tain't never gonna happen."

Roger said, "My head is killing me, I'm going try to get back to sleep, thanks for the water."

Kearns nodded, turned off the bright light, and laid back in the visitor's chair as Roger tried to find a comfortable position. As Roger sought the respite of sleep, he could not help but think of the chain of events that landed him in this hospital, cuffed to the bed and charged with murder. His mind drifted back to an afternoon in early spring when a phone call put the wheels in motion which transported him to this point. If you think about it, it is often just a phone call that changes our destiny..........

It was such a call on a sunny afternoon in January. As Roger Maynard returned from lunch, his secretary, said, "Mr. Newfeld called about ten minutes ago and he wants you to call him as soon as possible." Roger picked up his other messages and sat down at his desk. When Isaac Newfeld requested something as soon as possible, one would try to have done it yesterday. He was the principal owner and Chairman of the Board of the Sperling Mattress Company and a very impatient man. Roger dialed the corporate headquarters number and a pert voice greeted him, and asked how she might direct his call. When he told her that he was returning Mr. Newfeld's call, he was put through immediately.

"Hi Mr. Newfeld I got your message." "Roger, Roger, (Isaac Newfeld had a habit of invariably repeating a persons first name at the outset of a conversation) I need to have you come over to my office. Can you be here about 2:30, its very important." Roger said of course, and after ending the call he set about rearranging his afternoon schedule to accommodate the unplanned meeting he now had to attend. As he checked over production labor reports, he contemplated what the reason for his "summons" to headquarters might be. It could be something as trivial as a neon letter being out in the huge Sperling sign that decorated his plant when Mr. Newfeld passed the plant last night, to a major problem such as overall corporate profit margins dropping a couple percentage points.

Roger, an African American, was the Plant Superintendent of a sprawling mattress plant in Newark, and at thirty-eight still sported an athletic figure. He held an MBA from the Wharton School and had proven himself very competent in running a very efficient manufacturing operation. He was married to an amazing woman, Evona, and the father of an eleven year daughter, Lola, and a six year old son, Davon.

At one-thirty, Roger left his office and made the drive into the city, parked and was outside of Newfeld's office at 2:30. The secretary announced that Mr. Maynard was here, and Isaac Newfeld came out into the reception area outside of his office. He shook Roger's hand and placed an arm around his shoulder and said, "I'm glad you could make it. Come into the Board Room, we have some important business to discuss." As they entered the Board Room, Roger could see that the full Board of Directors was present. At such moments, Roger always felt a bit of apprehension, being the only black man in a room full of some of the most powerful white men in the industry.

Isaac Newfeld said, "Today, Sperling Mattress closed our acquisition of Southern Bedding. Because of tight security around our acquisition talks, I was unable to tell you about it. We are taking over their four plants and full distribution in six southern states. They have had great sales, but their costs have been burying them for the past several years. We, the Board, and myself have decided that what we need to make it a profitable, successful Sperling operation is a great Division Vice President of Operations. As a result, we want only the best, and who would be better than you Roger. In the four years you have been with us, you have strongly contributed to the most profitable period in our company's history."

Charlie Jacobs, one of the oldest Directors on the Board said, "Roger we have prepared what we feel is a generous salary package. Effective with your acceptance of the position, you will receive a $50,000 annual increase, taking you to $ 175,000 per year plus a very generous bonus or incentive plan which could earn you up to an additional $200,000."

At this point Isaac broke in, "Naturally, we will pay your complete relocation expenses, since you will have to move down there, and as a "promotion bonus" I want to give you a check for $ 25,000, for you and your family to use anyway you want. So what do you say?"

Roger answered, "For a change I am speechless and overwhelmed. I am deeply flattered by the confidence that you all have indicated with this proposal. I hope you understand that making such a move is a major event to a family; as a result I do want to discuss this with my wife and family before I give you a definite answer. I certainly have no question in my mind as to what I want to do, but Evona and I have been partners for fifteen years and I feel it only fair to have her participate in such an important decision."

Isaac Newfeld seemed a bit disappointed that Roger didn't hurry off to pack his bag, but he finally said "Well, that's fine Roger, we understand, take all the time you need, but let me know tomorrow morning." He smiled broadly and followed up his comment with "Just kidding, of course, but time is of the essence because now that I own those plants, everyday that you are not down there is costing me major dollars." Roger knew that the remark was not a joke as the four years he had spent with Isaac Newfeld taught him one thing… Isaac Newfeld never joked.

By three thirty in the afternoon, Roger had managed to catch up with Evvy, a nickname which Roger had come to use as often as "Honey" when addressing Evona. Evona worked as a Counselor for the Newark Department of Human Services and had just finished an interview in the North End office. During interviews with clients of the DHS, as it was referred to by employees, Evona would turn off her cell phone. She had no sooner turned it on when it chirped.

"Evvy, you won't believe what's happened, it's really wonderful news, but we need to have a long talk this evening. Can you call your Sister and see if she could pick the kids up and keep them overnight?"

Evvy asked, "Roger what is it, you sound so pumped up?" Roger was reluctant to break the news on the phone as he wanted to tell her face-to-face.

Roger responded, "Well I really don't want to discuss it on the phone. How soon could you be home?"

Evona said, "I will call Denora and see if she can watch the kids tonight. My last interview for the day is over and I'll pick up Lola and Davey up at the sitters and drop them at my Sisters if she can keep them. Big guy this had better be worth it."

Roger replied, "It is, just wait. I'm going to leave the office by four and come directly home. I'll see you then. Love you Babe." Evona said "Me too, see you soon at home."

As things worked out, Denora was able to keep the kids and Evona came in several minutes after Roger had arrived home. She found him at the kitchen window with a glass of ice tea in his hand staring vacantly outside. She put down her attaché case and purse on the counter and kissed him. "Ok, now what's with all the secrecy that we need to be alone? What is the big news?"

Roger said, "Be careful how you talk to a new Vice President." Evona could only manage "What?" "That's right I am, or shall I say can be, the Vice President of Operations for the Southern Division of Sperling Mattress Company."

Evona looked puzzled, "What is this "or can be" stuff", I don't understand."

Roger said, "That's what we have to talk about." This is contingent upon my, or I should say, our moving to South Carolina. This is a big decision for each of us and our kids. Before we talk about the pros and cons of that, let me tell you what this means financially."

Roger explained at length the salary increase, the incentive program, the promotion "bonus" Newfeld promised him, etc.

When he finished Evona's response was "Wow". "If only we didn't have to move. What do you think of moving down south?"

Roger said "I guess, to be honest, I have some concerns. Before I left my office I called Ken Grayson, you know the guy I play handball with every week. I knew that Ken had spent about five years in Charlotte for a European chemical company before they transferred him back to New York two years ago. I asked him how were race conditions down there, and would you believe he asked me."

"*You mean like NASCAR?*"

"I told him no, I mean like how is it between whites and blacks?"

He said "It's ok, you know its like up here there are some rednecks who have a thing about blacks, and there are also black militants who are always stirring something up. Why are you asking?"

"I told him about my promotion and that we are going to have to move down to the Greenville, North Carolina area to make it happen."

Ken said, "You and the family will love it. Everything is at a slower pace and the prices are at least one third lower down there for everything from housing to food."

"We chatted a bit more but that's the essence of what he told me."

Evona said, "Let's go out to dinner, I don't think well on an empty stomach."

Roger agreed and they had dinner at their favorite Italian restaurant, which was nearby. They didn't speak much about the decision, which faced them, as they were each absorbed in their own thoughts as to how this change would impact their lives.

After they were back in the car and returning home, Roger said, "You know if I don't make this move, I have to wonder what my future will be in the company. I know Newfeld will be mightily pissed that in effect I turned him down and perhaps caused him to lose money until he gets a good manager. Newfeld never forgets or forgives. I'm not really worried, with an MBA and being a minority, I feel certain that I could find an equal or maybe better position in a month or two, but I don't know if that's what I want."

Evona spoke up, "I want you and I, and of course the children, to be happy. This could be a major stepping-stone in your career. It could be a challenge for all of us, and the more I think about it, the more I feel we should go for it."

They arrived back home and sat up until one in the morning discussing the pros and cons of making the move. Roger had been away from his home in Pittsburgh and what family he had for over twenty years, since he was seventeen. It was far different for Evona. She had never lived outside of the Newark area. She had even commuted to Rutgers Brunswick campus where she majored in Social Sciences for her undergraduate degree and later for her Doctorate in Applied Psychology. In addition to her widowed mother, a sister, and a brother, she had numerous cousins, aunts and uncles in the immediate area. As Roger and Evona drew closer to a decision, their excitement grew over the prospects of a new life. When they finally did go to bed, sleep was long in arriving for each of them. When it did come, it was very restless.

For the first time in years, Roger's thoughts drifted back to a hot summer night when he was attending Pitt University in Pittsburgh. He had met a girl who was in her senior year at Carnegie Mellon, and after a great evening for a first date, he had dropped her at her home in McKeesport, just outside of Pittsburgh. Not having a car Roger had borrowed George Simons' BMW for the evening. As he stopped for a traffic signal, a car pulled up behind him. When the light changed, he started through the intersection when the vehicle behind him suddenly became illuminated with the traditional rotating blue and red flashing lights. He pulled to the curb on the opposite side of the intersection as the McKeesport police car pulled around him. A tall, thin police officer stepped from the cruiser and walked toward Roger as he unbuckled the cover of his holster.

Roger had opened his window as the officer approached and before he could ask what was wrong, the officer shining a flashlight in Roger's eyes, said, "Boy, I want to see your hands at all times. Now slowly get out of the car, give me your wallet and place both hands on the roof."

Roger said, "I don't know what's wrong, but whatever it is tell me."

The Officer said, "Listen boy, I'll ask the questions." Roger had slowly gotten out of the car, handed over his wallet, and placed his hands on the roof as instructed. The policeman was now behind Roger and he could smell the sour breath of the man. There was the smell of onions, probably from his dinner. He started to frisk Roger and as he did, he kicked Roger's ankle bones with the side of his boot and said, "Boy, I want you to spread em' and I mean now. What are you doing driving this here BMW? Don't tell me it's yours cause I already checked the registration, and that's not the name on your driver's license."

Roger responded that it belonged to "George Simons, a good friend at Pitt University."

The officer pushed Roger in the back and said "Look I don't want any of your lies and bullshit, I think you stole the car and you're probably dealing drugs, I'll betcha that if I search the car I'll find enough grass to get you on intent to distribute." Just at that moment another police car pulled up in back of the BMW and a heavy-set, Sergeant stepped out and walked up to them. He asked "Grimes, what have we got here?"

"Well sir, I think we may have ourselves car thief and maybe even a drug dealer. In any event, I think this Brother has done something."

The Sergeant took Roger's driver license from Officer Grimes and looked at it with a flashlight. He asked, "Are you by any chance the Son of Lieutenant Maynard from the 6th District PPD?"

Roger said, "Yes Sir, but he's in the 9th District."

The Sergeant said, "That's right it is the 9th District. Now what is this all about? Do you have a stolen report on this vehicle, Officer?" Roger interjected that he and George Simons were best of friends at the University and he had borrowed the car to take a date out for the evening. Grimes replied that they did not have any report but that he was going to check again. The Sergeant said, "Save your effort, this young man is alright, Let him go. I know his Father very well; I worked for him in the 9th for over three years before I came to McKeesport. I'll take full responsibility if it turns out to be any problem." Grimes was visibly displeased but he said, "If you say so Sergeant."

The Sergeant said, "Tell your Dad that Cliff Richards said hello and that we should get together some time. Don't pay any attention to Grimes, he's always looking for the big arrest." Roger thanked the Sergeant and mentally vowed never again to drive in McKeesport if he could help it. Of course, Roger had run into discrimination before, but never on this level. As he finally drifted off to sleep he could not help but have some concern. Roger sighed as he turned over to try to get to sleep. After all McKeesport, Pa. was certainly not the deep south.

At 9:00 A.M. the telephone on Isaac Newfeld's desk rang and the caller said, " We want to do it" Newfeld said, "Roger, Roger, I knew we could count on you." Roger pointed out that there was much planning to be done in order to make the transition on both ends smooth. Newfeld replied, "You draw up your plans and let me know when you'll be on line down south. I know you'll do your usual excellent job."

And so it was, that the die was cast and many lives would change forever. Like a pebble tossed into an ocean, no one knew what distant shores the ripples would eventually touch upon.

CHAPTER 2

The week that followed was hectic. Roger placed ads in the Wall Street Journal for an Operations Manager, his replacement, for the Newark plant. In addition he spoke with several of the "head-hunter" management placement firms to see if they had any likely candidates. His time frame was to hire his replacement within two weeks and have the individual on board within a month. Once this occurred Roger expected to stay active in the Newark Division for up to a month, unless he felt comfortable with his replacement sooner. During this period he also planned to make at least three or four visits to the newly acquired "Sperling-South Division", or "SSD" as it was being called within the company.

Roger had his secretary make the arrangements for his first visit and so on a bright, brisk morning, a week after he and Evvy had reached their decision, he strode out of the Greenville/Spartanburg airport. His agenda on this first trip was to meet the present management personnel and visit the four plants which comprised the SSD. Frank Bouchard, the Plant Superintendent of the Greenville Plant and Interim Operations Manager, met him.

The meeting bordered on humorous. Frank was of average build and height, graying at the temples. He was holding a sign "Sperling Mattress Co.", and as Roger approached him, Frank kept trying to move slightly to keep the main exit in his field of vision which was being blocked more and more as Roger approached. Finally standing directly in front of Frank, Roger said, "Frank Bouchard?"

Frank looked dumbfounded and managed to say "You're Roger Maynard? I mean Good Morning Mr. Maynard. Welcome to Greenville".

Roger said "Look I hope you and I are going to work very closely, so we may as well get it out in the open. You were expecting a white man, weren't you?"

Frank started to stammer and then said, "Yes, I was. I've spoken to you on the phone about five or six times since Sperling bought out the company and I never realized that you were black as you don't sound, well… black." He went on "Look I don't have a problem with that at all, its' just that it was sort of a shock. I'd be less than candid if I didn't tell you that there will be some that are going to have a problem with having a black in authority,"

As they pulled out of the parking lot their conversation continued. Roger told Frank, "That doesn't bother me as I expect a certain amount of resentment. I ran into it at the Newark plant when Mr. Newfeld first placed me in charge. I realize that some whites have never dealt with a black other than in a subordinate role, and this is probably a mild cultural shock. I asked you to set up a meeting for tomorrow morning with the Plant Managers and their Assistant Managers from the other three plants, is that set up?"

Frank answered that it was arranged, and that all would be present except for Jimmy Sills, the Assistant Plant Manager from the Cokely plant, as his Wife is being operated on tomorrow.

Roger said, "Make a note to have a nice flower or planter sent in the name of the company and post her hospital address on the bulletin boards in all plants."

Frank said, "Fine, I'll take care of it when we get to the plant. Unless you want some other order, I figured we would hit the Cokely plant first, then the Simpsonville plant, next the Highpoint plant, and finally we'll end up at the Greenville plant. It will be late, probably about 6:30 or 7:00. Your reservations are at the Hampton Inn, a short distance from the Greenville plant. I thought we could have dinner together, unless you prefer to dine alone."

Roger replied, "The itinerary sounds fine, I just want to get a quick look at the facilities so I have a little better feel for the operations. I would be delighted if you would join me for dinner, as I dislike eating alone."

The visits to the four plants went as scheduled. Roger met the Plant Managers, some of the Foremen, and other personnel. The atmosphere was very stiff and cold, and in more than a few instances he detected some raised eyebrows.

At dinner Roger said to Frank, "You know this is going to be more of a challenge than I anticipated. I felt some very hostile attitudes today. Like I said earlier it really doesn't bother me personally, but it certainly is going to add to the problems of meeting the mission and goals of the Company. In addition to this, some of the equipment I saw today is ancient, I don't know how you obtain the production levels that you do."

"Well, we meet the production schedules with a lot of overtime and overlooking some of the quality issues that crop up. As far as attitudes are concerned, it's pretty much as I predicted earlier today, but I think if you take the proper approach over a period of time, many will not even look at you as a black, but rather as the leader."

Roger thanked Frank for his confidence and they concluded their meal. Frank dropped Roger off at the motel and made arrangements to pick him up in the morning.

As the Plant Managers and their Assistants and key Foremen milled about in the hallway outside of the conference room having coffee and donuts, Roger was in a small kitchenette off to the side getting a sip of coffee before convening the meeting. He heard someone say, "Have you heard why they recommend burying Niggers at twelve feet deep rather than six foot deep for whites?" Another voice responded in the negative. The first voice replied, "Cause deep down they're good people." There was the sound of laughter and Roger stepped out into the hallway. The smiles disappeared from the men's faces as quickly as wallets at a pickpocket's convention.

Roger said, "Good morning. Its Bob Richardson from the Highpoint plant isn't it? I believe we met yesterday." As he said this, he extended his hand. Bob Richardson turned a shade or two whiter and nervously shook Roger's hand. Roger said, "Funny joke."

Richardson stuttered and twitched and said, "I really meant nothing by it. I mean I meant no harm to anyone. It was just something I heard."

Roger said, "Stick around for a few minutes after the meeting I want to see you in my office."

Frank called the meeting to order and introduced Roger. Roger stood and said, "I want to tell you who I am, what Sperling Mattress Company is about, and what to expect from the Company and myself, and finally what the Company and I expect from you. I'm thirty-eight years old, married to a wonderful woman and we have two great kids. I hail from Western Pennsylvania, just outside of Pittsburgh. I obtained my Bachelors Degree at Pitt University on an academic scholarship. While at Pitt I played on the basketball team, second string. I earned my Masters Degree in Business Administration at the Wharton School of the University of Pennsylvania. After college I worked as a Consultant for an investment capital group for several years, and then as a Plant Manager of a men's clothing factory for six years, moving up to Vice President of Manufacturing. It was following this that I joined Sperling Mattress and Isaac Newfeld, the President and Founder of Sperling Mattress Company. I've been in the bedding business for a little over four years and as you may have noticed, I'm Black. I know that this may offend some of your feelings about working for a Negro; however, you will find me no different than a man of any other race. I fervently hope that in a short while you will realize that you are not working *for* me, but rather *with* me."

"Enough about me, as I am sure we'll all get to know each other much better in the coming weeks and months." Roger then went on to give a brief history of the Sperling Mattress Company, how the company operates and its management policies and practices. Finally he outlined the profit and operational goals, and how each employee is expected to contribute a 110% effort to achieve those objectives. It was almost lunchtime when Roger concluded his prepared remarks and fielded questions from the group. Most of the questions related to benefits that they and all employees had accrued under the old owners and whether they would continue.

As Roger walked out of the conference room, he motioned to Bob Richardson to follow him. They went into Rogers's office that had been occupied by the previous owner and he asked Richardson to close the door.

"Mr. Maynard I'll just resign so you don't have to fire me."

Roger said, "Sit down and forget about resigning, I'm not going to fire you. Bob I've looked at the records of all of our middle management personnel, and your department has had the best production and cost results in the division. In addition the Highpoint plant seemed to be the cleanest and most orderly of all the plants I visited. What I want to say is that I enjoy a joke as much as the next man, but jokes that demean races and women are really not funny. They are cruel and tasteless. Do you really hate blacks? Do you know that joke wouldn't have been half as bad if you had not used the term "Nigger"?" Bob started to answer, but Roger said, "I don't expect you to answer that, but I do want you to take a fresh look at the world today. I want you to put yourself in the other man's shoes and try to understand his feelings and need for respect and dignity. Now if you think you can do that I want you go out of here and work at the things I told you. Can you do that?" Bob's face lit up and he replied that he was sure he could, enthusiastically shook hands with Roger and departed.

Roger asked for numerous files and documents to be sent to his Newark office so that he could review different areas of operations before his next visit. On the home front, he promised Evona that on his next visit he would take a day off to check on a potential residence, and the school situation. The search for his replacement was bearing fruit as he had three strong candidates that he had interviewed, and pending reference checks he would make a decision. The only downside following his return from his first visit was his briefing with Mr. Newfeld. Mr. Newfeld acted as though he had no intention of putting more capital into the new Division when Roger pointed out that it appeared over a million dollars was required for equipment replacement and plant modernization. As Roger told Mr. Newfeld, "This is just a preliminary estimate, I'll have a detailed capital budget on your desk within the next ten days. The Division cannot even start to meet our operational goals with equipment that is broke and out of service for an average of two days every week. You should have had me or our Plant Engineer go down and evaluate the equipment before you completed the merger." Newfeld's only comment was, "We shall see, we shall see."

CHAPTER 3

The following week all the pieces started to fall into place. After many interviews, Roger hired a gentleman named Charlie Cohen as the new Operations Manager for the Newark plant. His references were great and he had managed a large bedding operation in Los Angeles for three years, and the fact that he also possessed an MBA didn't hurt. He had introduced Charlie to Mr. Newfeld and the two hit it off like long time friends. Best of all was that he could start within the following two weeks.

With this task out of the way, Roger was able to concentrate on the reams of data that he had Frank send up to him. The more Roger looked at the data, the more he felt that poor management was not the reason that Southern States Bedding had been looking for a merger. There was definitely something very deceptive going on, or actually several things. Roger advanced his next visit by almost a week. He told Frank he was coming down a little earlier, and could he set up a meeting with Mr. Dave Atkins, the President of Great International Foam Corporation, a major supplier to the four plants.

Several days later Roger arrived at Greenville/ Spartanburg Airport, rented a car and headed to the Greenville plant. When he arrived, he huddled with Frank to outline his plans to update the equipment and bring the scheduling, accounting and operations into the computer age. Roger had been flabbergasted when he found out that the only usage of a computer in the entire operation was for payroll. He asked what time the trucks left for deliveries in the morning. Frank told him that trucks are loaded in the late afternoon and early evening of the previous day so that they could get on the road at five or six in the morning. Roger asked Frank if he could stay over this evening for a truck audit. Frank said it wasn't a problem, but that he would have to make a phone call to his wife.

By six-thirty that evening the last of the trucks were loaded and the dock crew left for the day. Roger asked Frank if the load documents were complete and Frank replied in the affirmative. Roger removed his coat and tie and said, "I haven't driven a forklift for over a year, but it's like riding a bike. Do you drive Frank?" Frank said he often drove in the plant when they were short-handed. They had three forty-five foot trailers and two local twenty-eight footers to check. A truck audit meant completely unloading and reloading while checking the cargo against the load manifest. Within an hour they had completed trailer one. The load had checked out exactly to the manifest. By nine o'clock they had finished the second trailer which contained eight mattresses over the paperwork; all were top of the line, expensive beds. The third trailer had one mattress over, which could be chalked up to human error, but it would be interesting to see if Larry Giles, the assigned driver reported it when he returned. The first straight truck checked out with three mattresses over. The second twenty-eight footer checked out one mattress short which turned up on the dock, a loading error for sure.

Frank asked what Roger wanted to do about this. Roger said, "Say nothing to anybody about this. We left the overage mattresses on the trucks so we'll see how honest our drivers are when they check in tomorrow afternoon. Do you completely trust the Plant Managers at the Cokely and Simpsonville Plants, as I want you to do the same checks at those plants tomorrow night? They only have two trucks at each plant. If you don't feel confident that you can trust either of the managers, let me know and I'll work with you, otherwise, I'll get Bob Richardson to help me at Highpoint as they have three trucks."

Frank, looked deep in thought, and finally said, "I guess the managers at those plants are reliable and honest, but I really can't say for sure. I just don't know them that well."

Roger said if Frank didn't feel one hundred percent confident, it would be best if they made the truck audits together. Roger pointed out that the loading personnel would be dealt with later as they had to be in collusion with the drivers.

The following morning the meeting with Dave Atkins took place. Frank introduced Dave to Roger, and Roger asked Frank to have Ray Crocker, the company's Purchasing Manager, to sit in on the meeting. Dave Atkins turned on all the "good-old boy" Southern charm that he could muster. Dave said, "I've heard a lot of good things about you Suh. It's a real pleasure to meet a man so well educated, and a real credit to his race."

Roger replied, "Sir, it is likewise a real pleasure to meet a man who can lay on compliments while he picks your pocket. And I'd like to know what "good things" you have heard about me?"

Dave Atkins stammered and huffed, "Well I cain't believe my ears, Suh. I came in here as a friend and key vendor to this company, and you choose to mimic and insult me. Why?"

Roger threw several packs of invoices on the table and said "You have been overcharging the previous company and now Sperling Mattress Company 15 to 20 % over the going price of foam in this market. In addition I had samples of your foam tested and they averaged fifteen percent under weight on the density. Suh, you have been stealing from us and causing us costly warranty problems with your under spec. foams. As if this is not enough to sate your greed, I checked your last shipment which came in yesterday afternoon and found it to be short three rolls of quilting foam although your delivery receipt showed the full amount. Of course, this is a situation that should have been caught by our receiving clerk; a problem that I can assure you will be taken care of. I want to be the first to inform you that you are no longer our supplier, and when I dig into this further, I will forewarn you that there may be a lawsuit in your future. I believe that concludes our business here. It was a "real pleasure" to have met you "Suh".

As Dave Atkins picked up his briefcase he said "We should speak in private Mr. Maynard" Roger replied "That would be a waste of our time" Dave Atkins shook his head and left.

Roger turned to Ray Crocker and said, "Ray we are not going to prosecute you for collusion to defraud the company, but you are hereby discharged. I had an independent investigator check you out and it seems that every time the company pays an invoice to Atkins, several days later you deposit $ 1000.00 in your bank account. Also, your wife doesn't work and you earn only $30,000 per year but you live in a $250,000.00 home with a mortgage payment of just under $2000.00 per month. I just don't know how you make ends meet. Our decision to not prosecute you hinges on your giving testimony against Atkins, if we do proceed with a lawsuit".

Ray squirmed in his chair, loosened his tie and opened his collar. In a rather shrill voice he said, "Look, I'm not going to be the fall guy for this. Yes, I was getting a thousand from Mr. Atkins, but that was nothing to what Mr. Austin was receiving. I betcha that he was getting something like five or ten thousand dollars every time from Atkins."

Roger interrupted, "Now you are referring to Mr. Elwood Austin, the previous owner of this company?"

Crocker mumbled, "That's right, cuz sometimes Mr Atkins would give me an envelope for Mr. Elwood, and it would feel five or six times heavier than mine."

Roger asked, "Did you actually see money in those envelopes?"

Crocker said, "Can't you reconsider, I need this job, I'll tell you whatever I can, I can be a good employee, you can trust me."

Roger looked at Frank and said, "Do you believe this?" Turning his attention back to Ray Crocker, Roger said, "No, I would never feel comfortable with you working here. Now tell me when did you last get an "envelope" from Dave Atkins, and did you ever see cash in the envelopes that Atkins gave to Mr. Austin? If you want two weeks severance pay and a clean reference, you'll answer now and truthfully."

Ray Crocker sighed and said, "About three years ago, I went to Mr. Austin and asked him why don't we buy our foam cheaper because other foam companies have talked to me and offered much better prices. Mr. Austin told me "Don't get involved in the foam area because he took care of that personally and that I should just place the orders for what the plants need, and forget about it."

"Well about a week later Mr. Atkins came by to see Mr. Austin and he stopped in my office to see me. He says, "Elwood was telling me that you are concerned about our prices." Then he says, "Well Ray, my boy, you take this and they'll be more where this came from, just keep up the good work." He handed an envelope to me and it had five hundred dollars in it. Then Mr. Atkins says, "Elwood's secretary tells me that Elwood is gone for the day so hang onto this envelope for him and give it to him in the morning." He patted me on the back and left. The next morning when Mr. Elwood came in, I followed him to his office and told him that Mr. Atkins asked me to give the envelope to him. Mr. Elwood nodded, took the envelope and ran his finger up under the sealed flap and I could see that there was cash inside. He didn't take it out, so I don't know what denomination the bills were."

"Around eighteen months ago, Mr. Atkins gave us a big price increase because it seemed like the whole industry was raising prices and I said to Mr. Atkins that the other foam companies were only raising their prices by less than half of his increase. He said', "Ray you worry too much", and the next envelope had a thousand dollars, and when he handed it to me he said "Don't worry anymore, worrying can be bad for your health." The last envelope he brought by was last week."

Frank said, "I spoke to Elwood about the foam prices and the quality problems, and he just told me the same thing, "don't worry about it. I take care of our foam purchases."

Ray said, "See it's just like I told you, this all just happened, and I was in the middle. Please reconsider and give me a second chance"

Roger responded, "If you had refused the money from Atkins, you would still have your job, but you had to know that kickbacks are illegal, I'm sorry. We will give you a glowing letter of reference, I'll mail it to you in a few days."

Roger told Frank to go with Ray and have him clean out his office of anything personal and leave the premises. They would just tell the rest of the staff that Ray was laid off as a new purchasing agent was coming in from Sperling headquarters. Actually this was not far from the truth as Roger had hired an accounting/computer guru who was now training at the Newark plant to become totally knowledgeable of Sterling's accounting programs.

Frank came into Roger's office to report that Ray Crocker had left the premises saying he would testify if necessary, but muttering that some day he would "get even with that black bastard for not giving him a second chance."

Roger nodded and asked Frank to close the door and sit down. Frank said, "I guess its' my turn now, although I don't know of anything that I did."

Roger shook his head and said, "Frank, it's not anything that you've done, but rather what you have not done. With so many glaring problems, you either chose to close your eyes, or else you're incompetent which I don't feel is the case. What's the story Frank?"

Frank looked at Roger and shook his head and he didn't say anything for over a minute. Finally he said, "Look, I know it's not in my personnel records which I am sure you have reviewed, but I'm an alcoholic. I've been sober now for the three years that I have been with Southern Bedding and now Sperling. I had been fired from my last two jobs as Plant Manager with two different mattress manufacturers. Oh, they liked me and the job that I was capable of doing, but they just couldn't tolerate the days when nobody could find me, not even my wife, the missed meetings, the schedule screw-ups that I made while bombed. So they let me go with good references and recommendations."

Mr. Austin had an opening here at the Greenville plant and he took a chance on me because my wife had gone to school with his wife. I started attending AA meetings, found God, and I've been sober since. Well, a short time after I was here, I noticed different things that just didn't seem right, and some I corrected and others I reported to Mr. Elwood. A short time after that Elwood called me here into this very office, which was his, and gave me holy hell; he said you just keep the plant running and get the production out. He said don't get involved with accounting, purchasing, or sales. He reminded me of the possibility that I could be without a job. As a result I did exactly what you said, I closed my eyes and my ears. I cannot afford to lose this job. It would devastate my wife. I'm forty-five years old and I don't know if I could find another opportunity to start over."

Roger said, "That's all I wanted to know, but I'm telling you right now, open your eyes and keep them open. I'm counting on you to be a key player on our team, and I want to feel that I have your complete support. You've been around and you know the mattress business, I want you to think in terms of the total picture. I'm going to assume that you're off the sauce for good. Manage like it's your money and your own the business."

Frank replied, "Like I told you, I've been sober for three years now and I can tell you that I will do everything possible to maintain my sobriety. I still attend as many AA meetings as possible. As far as supporting you, you have my word, which I hope as you get to know me better will, mean something to you. We've only known each other for a short time, but you have shown that you are fair and a man of your word and you are very competent in your position."

Roger thanked Frank and reminded him that they had some trucks to check in later that day. As Frank started to leave Roger's office he paused and said "Oh, by the way, I fired one of our tape edgers, Jamie Williams, this morning, and he is insisting that he talk to you. I told him that wouldn't be possible, but before I came in, he was still in the employee lunchroom waiting to see you. Should I call the sheriff's office and have him escorted off?"

Roger said "No, I'll see him. What did you fire him for?" Frank replied, "Unexcused absences, lateness, insubordination, and you name it. Let me get you his employment folder as everything is documented, and it will help you in talking to him." Within a few minutes, Frank was back and gave Roger the folder.

After Roger reviewed it, he ask his secretary to page Mr. Jamie Williams to come to the office, and shortly a tall, lanky black man walked into Roger's office. Roger said "Mr. Williams I understand that you have been terminated by Mr. Bouchard. What is it you wish to speak to me about?"

Jamie shifted from one foot to the other and looking down at the edge of the desk he said "Well Mr. Roger, I knows that Mr. Frank doesn't lak me and he try evry thang to fire me. I wanted to ask you bein a Brothah an all that, if you could get me a second chance, you know..."

Roger had held his hand up and said, "Mr. Williams, don't even try to go there, I am not your Brother, and I don't care if you're purple. When we hired you it was because we need you in the position that you held. We depend on you being here when you are scheduled to work, not the next day or three hours late. I've reviewed your record, and I support Mr Bouchard's decision 100%. Now please leave the premises, your check will be mailed to your residence the end of this week. If you don't leave now, we'll call the authorities and have you escorted off of company property."

Jamie glared at Roger and said "Man! Yo ain't nothin but a damn Uncle Tom. I tol all the Brothahs in the plant that I didn't trust you, and I right. Don't get worried Man, I'm leaving now, but I'll talk to yo agin sometime when yo not behind that desk." With that Jamie Williams turned and left.

Late in the afternoon the delivery trucks returned and Larry Giles, the driver, reported one mattress over and returned. Roger and Frank waited for Roland Grimes with three mattresses over, and Sam Rosallo with eight mattresses over to come in. Finally a little after five both drivers pulled in within five minutes of each other. Frank stopped Roland on the dock and asked, "Where are the three mattresses you were over without any delivery ticket?" Roland was visibly shaken as he managed to say "Wha, What three mattresses?" Frank told him that it was the three he had sold under priced and pocketed the cash. Again Roland denied it, but when Frank told him he was lying because he and Roger had personally counted the load and compared it to the manifest, Roland said "Hey, look I remember I sold them to one of our dealers and he gave me the cash to turn in." Frank merely shook his head and said, "Nice try, but you're fired, go clean out your locker. We're not going to press charges unless you give us further reason to do so." Roland was on the verge of tears and he nodded and went in to clean out his personal items.

Roger and Frank both confronted Sam Rosallo after he checked in, the conversations went much the same except Sam continued to deny that he had any merchandise on his truck that was not covered by a delivery manifest. Rosallo had been with the previous company for almost five years and there were rumors that his brother and several other relatives were involved in the rackets in the Charlotte area. He accused Maynard of wanting to get rid of all the "white guys" in the company and to replace them with "the brothers" as he phrased it. Overall it was an ugly discharge and it left Roger apprehensive about the further ill will that could be spread with Rosallo's accusation. Roger instructed Frank to hire two new drivers asap and to make sure that they were white. Frank agreed although he thought Rosallo's comment was his opinion and his alone and that it did not reflect the feelings of other personnel.

Frank and Roger locked up the plant and Roger said he was going to just grab a quick meal at Dennison's, a local supper club near his motel. "It's been a tough couple of days,

Frank, and I know you're tired and you should get home to your family. I've got to meet with a realtor tomorrow morning to see if I can find a place and bring my family down. Then I have an early afternoon flight back to Newark, so I'll only be in the office for a short while." Frank said goodnight and Roger pulled out of the office parking lot. He was deep in thought and tired, so he didn't notice a car pulling out from curbside further down the street and take up a position a half block in back of his car.

Roger pulled into the parking lot at Dennison's and was soon seated at a table in the dining room. He ordered and was waiting for his salad when a very attractive, light skinned, Negro woman approached his table. She was well dressed and carried a drink from the bar. "Hi, I know you don't know me, but I bet I know you."

Roger looked up from a report he was reading and said, "You are correct, I don't know you."

The woman said, "I think you're that new manager from the mattress factory, cause I have friends that work there and they tol me bout you. Could I sit here at your table with you?" Roger replied that he did not mind and asked if the woman lived in the area and did she have a name. She said her name was Hanna and that she was from Spartanburg. Roger asked if he could buy her dinner but she declined saying that she had eaten earlier, but that he could buy her a drink.

The conversation was light and touched on the weather, how friendly everyone was, etc. Roger asked about where the best schools were, where was a good area to live, etc. By the time Roger finished his dinner and Hanna had consumed two vodka gimlets, Hanna said, "Look the night is young and my car is in a shop, so I have no place to go and I could go to your room with you and give you more information, and anything else you may want."

Roger said "Look Hanna, I enjoyed talking to you and appreciate the information that you gave me, but I don't think it would be appropriate for you to be in my motel room. You're very attractive, and if I were a single man I would welcome your company, but I have a wonderful wife and great family. I think it's best that I say it was a pleasure meeting you, and I hope you understand my position, so I will say goodnight."

Hanna said, "Well you don't know what you all is gonna miss, but if that's the way you all wanna be then I'll say, thanks for the drinks and goodnight also." Immediately after Roger pulled out of the lot, Hanna exited the club and held a cell phone to her ear. She said only a few words, "Forget it, he's a real boy scout, so take your camera home."

CHAPTER 4

At nine o'clock the intercom on Roger's desk announced that a Ms. Atwater was here for an appointment. This was the realtor, and Roger left with her to view homes in the area. She showed him several homes that were adequate, but not quite what he and Evvy wanted. In addition Ms. Atwater said that, "One neighborhood was rumored to have drug problems at the local school, and that the other neighborhood, while it looked nice, was noted for red-necks." Finally, she said, "I know where I have a home that's empty and ready for immediate occupancy. It's in one of the best neighborhoods in the area with great schools, and mostly all professional people and local executives. It also has five bedrooms, four and a half baths, a huge family room with a real fireplace, an in ground pool and just about everything else that you and your wife seem to be looking for. Best of all its priced at almost a hundred and fifty thousand under the current market prices."

Roger said "Gee it sounds great, why didn't you show it to me first? If it's everything you say, we could have saved each other some time."

Ms. Atwater sighed and said, "Well, I was told that I should only offer it to white, professional clients, but this is my last week in this town as we're moving down to Atlanta. I really don't care because I know that several of those people in Glenwood Commons blackballed my husband's and my application for membership in the Country Club, and I think it's time they entered the 21st century."

"Look, I don't want my family and I to be "block-busters", that's a term that we used up North for when blacks started integrating all white neighborhoods." Roger pointed out.

"Oh, I know you won't have any problem once they get to know you. These are well educated, civil people, not the Klan." Roger agreed to look at the property, but made no further commitment,

The house was a beautiful brick and stone rancher set on an acre and a half lot, beautifully landscaped with numerous shade trees. It had a pool and spa in the rear. As Mrs. Atwater had said, it was empty and she was correct; it had everything that Roger and his wife wanted in a home. The house was immaculate and priced at three hundred thousand, well below market for a quick sale. Roger made an offer of $ 10,000 less and wrote a check for a deposit, and signed a contract of sale contingent on Evvy's approval. Roger had his cell phone - camera with him and took numerous shots to show Evvy.

CHAPTER 5

It was a Friday afternoon and the Greenville-Spartanburg Airport was bustling with businessmen on their way home to wherever. Maynard checked in and took a seat near the announced gate. The Eastern flight to Newark was delayed as it was held in Birmingham due to bad weather. Finally it arrived and the plane was packed. Roger thought I hope Evvy likes the house, because I don't want to make many more of these trips.

Things did not improve as Newark also had storms and heavy rains, and the plane was in a stack pattern for over a half hour. The airport itself was a mad house and his luggage was forever coming up on the belt. Once it arrived, he called Evvy and told her where to pick him up, and in ten minutes he was placing his luggage in the trunk of her car. He kissed her as he took the driver's seat, and carefully pulled out into the traffic flow. He reached into his coat pocket and removed his cell phone, handed it to Evvy and told her to bring up his photos.

After a minute or two, she exclaimed, "Oh my God, this is the house you told me about?"

Maynard said, "It sure is and unless you disapprove, we are on our way to becoming its new owners, as I put a deposit on it this morning." Evvy excitedly held the phone up for the children to see as she told them "Look it even has an in ground swimming pool. No more going over two miles to a community pool." The kids joined in the excitement and were bouncing up and down on the back seat. Evvy said, "Get those seat belts back on and behave yourselves. I know you're excited but let's not act crazy." With this Lola and Davon settled down for the half hour drive home.

As they pulled into their driveway, the rain started again with a real cloud burst. By the time Evvy got her umbrella open, she and the kids were half drenched. They rushed into the house and Roger said he would retrieve his luggage from the car when the rain stopped. They sent out for pizza and spent the evening talking about their new home, and where their furniture would be placed, what additional furniture they would require, and all of those other myriad details connected with the move.

About 9:00 o'clock in the evening, the phone rang, it was Mrs. Atwater. She said, "I have wonderful news for you, the owners didn't accept your offer, but they counter proposed that they would meet you halfway and knocked the price down by $5000. Is that acceptable to you?"

Roger smiled and said, "Yes. I'll be back in Greenville on Tuesday, and yes I will try to see if my wife can fly down to sign the loan application." The conversation ended with Mrs. Atwater's arrangements to meet them at the airport.

So ended a day which was started with a promise and ended with the promise fulfilled, or at least heading in that direction.

CHAPTER 6

Evvy spent several hours on the phone Saturday speaking with her supervisor and a few clients rearranging her schedule so that she could accompany Roger on Tuesday. Finally all necessary arrangements were made including having her sister take care of the kids on Tuesday and Wednesday when she would return. The rest of the weekend passed quietly with evaluating what had to be done to the house before they could put it on the market.

Five years before, they had purchased the home for just over two hundred and eighty thousand, and they had spent another twenty thousand on extensive remodeling. Roger did a great deal of the work himself as he was very handy with tools. They had talked briefly with a realtor and he felt they could expect to sell it for three hundred and ten plus.

One thing they decided was that the children's rooms needed repainting, and that they would put down a ceramic tile floor in the kitchen.

Sunday, the family went to Home Depot to pick out the paints and the tile. Lola and Davon were becoming more and more excited about the pending move, and it filled most of the hours of family conversation.

Monday started out humid and overcast with threat of thunder storms in the afternoon. Charlie Cohen had started a week earlier and was getting well into his position.

Things were going very well at the Newark plant and Roger breathed a sigh of relief.

Roger had a meeting scheduled with Mr. Newfeld to update him on progress at the Southern Division. Roger wished to go ahead with a law suit against Atkins, but this was something that required Newfeld's approval. Roger assured Newfeld that they had an excellent case of collusion. Issac gave his OK and said he would contact Sperling's law firm, and have them get in touch with Roger to get the process started.

They discussed numerous other aspects of the Southern Division operations, and Issac clapped Roger on the shoulder and said he felt Roger was doing an excellent job. Roger told Mr. Newfeld that he found a property for sale in Greenville. and hopefully would have his family moved down with him within the next two months if not sooner. Issac thought this was great and looked forward to visiting the plants that he had acquired and meeting some of the key people "down there."

CHAPTER 7

Roger and Evvy had an early morning flight out of Newark with a half hour stopover in Charlotte. The flights were smooth and on time, a real accomplishment for Eastern. As scheduled, Mrs. Atwater met them in the Greenville airport and they set off to visit what Roger hoped would be their new home. Evvy was impressed with the fresh appearance of the area and the lack of bumper to bumper traffic. Spring did it's thing in this area about a month before Newark and the Mid-Atlantic Area. Trees were fully leafed out and flowers were in full bloom everywhere.

Evvy loved the house at first sight from the driveway, and the interior literally entranced her.

After an hour of looking inside and out, there was no doubt that this was the home for Evvy and her family. Mrs. Atwater had loan applications for four banks in the area and recommended Southern States Banking and Trust as they were several tenths of a percent lower than the rates of the other three banks. Roger asked Mrs. Atwater to drop them at the Alamo Car Rental office. As they were walking out to the driveway, they noticed that there was a woman on the porch of the house next door, and she called to Mrs. Atwater, who muttered, "What does she want now?" as she motioned Roger and Evvy into her car.

Roger and Evvy watched as the neighbor and Mrs. Atwater engaged in an animated discussion. Finally Mrs. Atwater put her hands in the air and quickly walked over to the car. Evvy asked if anything was wrong as Mrs. Atwater seemed agitated. She said, "No. That woman, Mrs. Ward, is a very nice person, but she is a worry wart, always checking to make sure I locked up the house good and whatever else she can think of to complain about."

Evvy asked "Is there going to be a problem because we're a black family?"

Mrs. Atwater replied, "I do not think it is going to be a problem any more so than any new family moving into a long settled neighborhood. People don't know you and they are a little apprehensive until they get to know you." Mrs. Atwater took them to the Alamo car rental at the airport and said she would notify them when settlement would take place.

The loan application at the bank went smoothly. Roger and Evvy were in and out in less than an hour. It was early afternoon and Evvy asked Roger not to go into the office as he was planning. The day was bright and spring was bursting out in its full glory everywhere one looked. Evvy asked, "When was the last time we had a free afternoon just to ourselves with no kids and nothing to do and no place to go? Let's go to your motel." Roger did not have to be asked twice. With his schedule of being away for a week or two at a time, their sex life had suffered. They entered his room at the Southern Comfort Inn, and immediately became locked in an intense embrace. As they kissed, their tongues found each other. By the time they undressed, Evvy and Roger were ready. It was like the sex of their honeymoon which was now such a distant memory. They made love several times and dozed in between.

As light was beginning to fade outside, they showered and got dressed, Roger called and made reservations at the finest restaurant in Greenville, the Golden Calf. When they arrived the Maitre Dei seemed a bit taken back, but he quickly subdued his surprise that they were black, and seated them toward the rear of the dining room. Their waiter was a middle aged black gentleman, dressed immaculately in a tux, who introduced himself as George.

The service was excellent and the food was as great as Evvy or Roger had ever enjoyed anywhere. They had just finished their appetizers when Evvy looked up and said, "Roger would you believe that Mrs. Ward and, I guess, her husband just came in and are being brought to the only empty table here which is next to ours."

Roger asked "You mean our new next door neighbor?" "It's the only Mrs. Ward that I know" Evvy responded. As they were being seated, Mrs. Ward glanced at the adjoining table and that momentary flicker of recognition crossed her face. She was a few feet away from Evvy and her husband was facing toward Roger. Roger nodded slightly and Mr. Ward did likewise, as two strangers, like business men might do when encountering each other in a line at the airport.

Evvy leaned toward Mrs. Ward and said, "Hello Mrs. Ward, I don't mean to be forward, but it does seem we are going to be neighbors." Mrs Ward was a middle-aged woman probably in her late forties or early fifties as near as Evvy could estimate. She was tastefully dressed and her husband was dressed in a suit and tie as was Roger. Mrs. Ward seemed a little startled and registered surprise, but she cleared her throat and said, "You're correct, it does seem that way." Evvy replied, "My name is Evona Maynard, Evvy for short, and this is my husband Roger Maynard."

Mrs. Ward replied that her name is Elizabeth and her husband is Henry Ward. Roger said he was very pleased to meet them and stood and reached across the table to shake hands with Mr. Ward, who also stood. At that point, Evvy and Roger's entrees were served and they directed their attention to eating the most astonishing steaks they ever had. The Wards in the meantime perused their menus and ordered. They obviously had skipped the appetizer course and had ordered the special of the day as their food was served quickly and they practically finished dining about the same time as Roger and Evvy.

Roger asked Mr. and Mrs. Ward if they would join them for coffee and possibly a desert. Mr. Ward shot a glance at his wife and hesitated a second and said "Yes, we would be delighted to." George cleared their table and the Wards seated themselves at Evvy and Roger's table. George came back to take their orders. All declined deserts and they all ordered coffees except for Mrs. Ward who ordered tea. Mr. Ward asked where are you folks from and Evvy answered New Jersey. The next question was what brings you folks to Greenville? Roger gave a brief summary of the Sperling Mattress Company acquisition of Southern States Bedding Company, and his role as Chief Operating Officer and Vice President. Evvy came into the conversation and provided a bit about her background as a Counselor in the New Jersey Department of Human Service, She also felt it wouldn't hurt to mention that she held a Doctorate degree in Applied Psychology. She also added that Roger held an MBA from the Wharten School of the University of Pennsylvania.

Mr. Ward asked Roger when did he attend Wharten as he attended only one year. He related that he dropped out when his father passed away, and he finished his MBA at U of South Carolina. Roger told him the dates of his attendance at Wharten. It was over a decade of difference in their dates of attendance, but they were able to remember certain professors who each of them were familiar with. Mrs. Ward asked if they had any children and Evvy took the opportunity to pull out her wallet pictures of Lola and Davon. The Wards had finished their beverages as had Roger and Evvy. Mr. Ward related that he is presently teaching at the Greenville-Spartanburg Community College and he is the Department Head of the Department of Commerce and Industry, but that after four years he has tired of teaching and academia, and has been putting out feelers in local industry. He went on to say, "I'm awfully glad to have met you, and to get to know you folks. I'll tell you, we, Mrs. Ward and I, were a little apprehensive about suddenly having black neighbors. I hope you understand we just didn't know what to expect, but you are both very well educated and refined." Roger was about to ask "What did you expect, a drug dealer or rapist?", but he changed his mind as he appreciated the honesty of Mr. Ward, besides he had taken a quick liking to the man.

Evvy and Roger felt that meeting with the Wards had been a fortuitous bit of fate, as they were probably somewhat accepted by at least one neighbor. However, as they drifted off to sleep both of them knew that they probably had an uphill effort on their hands,

CHAPTER 8

Evvy had an early morning flight back to Newark, and by 7:00 AM they left the motel for the airport. They had coffee and danish in the coffee shop at the airport and by then it was time for Evvy's flight. They embraced at the gate and sadly Evvy's visit was over.

Roger drove to the plant, entered his office, and paged Frank to come to his office. A few minutes later a very harried looking Frank entered and announced that number two quilting machine had been broken down since yesterday, and production schedules were shot to hell. Roger asked if there were any other problems. Frank said other than having to fire one of the forklift drivers for showing up under the influence, things were running OK. Roger said, "Let's take a look at that quilter, I'm not a mechanic but sometimes another set of eyes can help."

They entered the plant and as they approached the number two quilter, Smitty, the operator crawled out from the underside of the machine, followed by Drake the plant mechanic. "The entire timing mechanism is screwed up, that's why it won't sew!" Drake announced.

Roger said, "If my memory serves me, I believe that the looper timing is controlled by a gear assembly here on the front side of the machine. Have we taken that apart?" Drake said, "No Sir, I was tied up on fixing one of the dock doors most of yesterday, so they could get trucks in and out. This the first chance I've had to look at it." Drake removed the gear case cover which is held in place by a pair of thumb screws. The four men almost as one said, "There it is!!" A mangled steel washer was locked between the gear teeth.

Frank asked, "Could it have fallen off of any bolt and fell in there by itself?" Drake shook his head and said, "I can't see any way that that could happen, it had to be put in there by someone." Roger asked Smitty, 'Were you in the vicinity of the machine all of yesterday?" Smitty thought for a moment and replied, "Yeah, except for lunch time when I shut down the machine and went outside to eat my lunch. While I was here I didn't see anyone around the quilter. It was runnin fine in the mornin, but right after lunch is when it messed up." Drake said, "I think someone sabotaged it." Frank told Drake and Smitty to get it fixed asap, and if they needed any parts, to order them with FedEx overnight delivery.

As Frank and Roger walked through the plant, Roger remarked, "Great, this equipment is being held together with baling wire and duct tape, and now, someone is shutting it down with junk"

Frank said "I'll catch the son of a bitch if it's the last thing I do, and it will be no more Mr. Nice Guy. I'll have them prosecuted."

Roger asked what time did Frank fire the forklift driver. He replied, "It was about quarter to twelve as he came in late and one of the guys on the dock came to me to tell me he thought something was wrong with Bobby Joe. I immediately went out to the dock and found him sitting in the forklift with his eyes closed. I ordered him off of the lift and asked him to walk a straight line, and a few other tests. He failed all of them, and I looked closely at his eyes which were quite dilated. At that point I told him he was fired and to clean out his locker. I had him sit in my office and I typed up a statement of the incident and of his discharge, and I had him sign it. He denied that he was under the influence, but finally he signed it." Roger then asked, if to Frank's knowledge, did Bobby Joe ever work on or around the quilter. Frank said he would check and get back to Roger.

CHAPTER 9

Roger had numerous tasks facing him, and he went to his office to get started on reviewing purchase orders, signing checks, and scanning last week's sales and production reports for signs of problems. An hour and a half passed quickly when the phone rang. Daisy, the receptionist, announced that a Ms. Hanna Williams was waiting to see him and that she apologized for not making an appointment. Roger inquired what company did she represent? There was a pause and the receptionist returned to say she represents the Carolina Foam Industries. This was a Dave Atkins company which was banned from the company premises. Roger said, "Send her in."

As Daisy led Ms. Williams into Roger's office, he immediately recognized her as the Hanna he had met over a month ago as he had dinner. The woman who had invited him to her motel. Hanna said, "I'm so sorry that I didn't call for an appointment, but I was in this end of town and I thought I would see if you had a few minutes."

Roger said, "So you represent Dave Atkin's company?"

Hanna replied, "that she started as a Sales Representative a few weeks ago and she would really like to get the account back."

Roger asked, "Did Mr. Atkins tell you to call on me?"

Hanna shook her head and said, "No, I knew we had lost your account, and I just thought maybe we could work out the problems and do business again." Roger motioned for her to sit and as she did, she flashed a large amount of thigh. She was a very attractive woman whose skin color was almost the same as Evvy's.

Roger said, "I will tell you right up front, there is no way that we are doing any business with Carolina Foam Industries, now or ever. We have evidence that Mr. Atkins is quite dishonest on a number of levels, and we will probably meet in court at some point in the future. Now if there is nothing else that I can do for you, we should conclude this meeting. I'm very busy."

Hanna rose and extended her hand which Roger took. She said, "Why don't you let me take to you dinner this evening? I have an expense account and I really have to use it to show that I am doing my job and trying to obtain customers." Roger said, "Thank you anyway, but it would be most inappropriate in view of our relationship with Mr. Atkins. Besides, as I told you before, I am a happily married man and I intend to keep it that way."

Hanna, bent to pick up her brief case and she said with a grin, "Mr. Maynard, I do believe that you are frightened of me."

Roger responded, "Not as much as I am frightened of myself." With that Roger held the door and Hanna left.

Frank, looked in and while standing in the doorway of Roger's office he said, "I checked Bobby Joe's employment record with the company," Roger motioned Frank to come in and shut the door. Frank proceeded to tell Roger that, "Bobby Joe had a spotty record with the company.

He was employed several years before I joined the company as a helper on local deliveries, but after drivers complained that he was lazy and more of a hindrance than a help, they moved him into the plant. Guess where they put him to work? With Smitty on the quilter to train as a backup operator. That only lasted about two months, when Smitty complained that he was lazy and slow. After that he was put on the forklift to load trucks and move materials around the plant. He was suspended five times over the last few years for absenteeism, failure to call in, lateness, etc. I think we have found our saboteur. Should I swear out a warrant and have him arrested?"

Roger said, "I would like to, but it may just stir up more bad feelings in the plant just when things seem to be settling down. He's gone let's drop it." Frank nodded and excused himself to get back on the factory floor.

The balance of the afternoon passed quickly and at five thirty, Roger found himself with more reports and memos yet to review. He and Frank locked up and called it a day at least until Roger got to the motel to finish the paperwork he had stuffed in his briefcase. As he sat in the restaurant, waiting for his meal he called Evvy. She had gotten back to Newark and went to her office for a few hours before picking up the kids at her sister's. She said Lola and Davon had a million questions ranging from how deep is the pool, to can we have chickens and rabbits?

After dinner he started on his paperwork and before he knew it, it was almost 11:00 and time for news. He changed into his pajamas and sat in the one comfortable chair in the room and turned on the TV. As the news was starting, the phone on the nightstand rang. It was the front desk and the night clerk informed him that he had a guest. Roger asked who it was and the clerk answered, "She says she's a Ms. Hanna Williams." Roger replied, "Tell her if she needs to contact me, she can call me at my office tomorrow" and he hung up.

There was an uneasy feeling that something was going on, or perhaps some sort of set up, but there was nothing he could do about it. Hanna Williams was certainly trying to worm her way into his life, but why? After the news, he fell asleep with that question on his mind, and a determination to stay as far away as possible from Ms. Williams.

In the morning Ms. Atwater called to tell him that settlement was in three weeks at the bank's office at 10:30 AM. The really good news was that they could move in immediately after settlement. With that goal in mind the next several weeks flew by with weekends being spent in Newark getting the house ready for sale and packing. After two weeks of packing and repainting, the house was turned over to a realtor with an asking price of $325,000. Neither Evvy or Roger thought they would get that, but the second weekend a couple signed a contract for the full asking price. It seems that they needed a place in the Newark area at once and since the Maynards were going to be out in a few days, it made the sale. A quick settlement date was set and in a few days the movers came.

CHAPTER 10

The move went smoothly and Roger now had Evvy and his children with him. They moved in on a Friday and also had some new pieces of furniture delivered the same day, namely a new living room set. About 11:00 Saturday morning the chimes announced someone at their front door. It was a couple who introduced themselves as Susan and Ellwood Wedders; their other next door neighbors. Susan had baked a pound cake and brought it over as a welcome to the neighborhood token. They appeared to be in about the same age bracket as Roger and Evvy.

Evvy invited them to stay and have coffee and some of the delicious looking pound cake. Davey and Lola came up out of the basement where they had been working on unpacking toys and sorting them out into a closet filled with shelves. Evvy introduced the children who, thank goodness, were on their best behavior. The Wedders said that they had two children also, a boy seven, and a girl thirteen going on twenty. They were originally from Syracuse, New York, and had moved down eight years ago when the company Ellwood worked for moved their plant to Spartanburg. The meeting was very cordial and sort of like a "fact finding" mission for both couples. The Wedders said they were glad to see a little diversity in the neighborhood as there are few "rednecks" on the block.

Other than the dinner meeting, Evvy had seen Mrs. Ward out tending to her garden a few times and had several very brief conversations. Things at the plant seemed to improve and Roger got to know everyone by their first name. Some of the earlier personnel problems disappeared and Frank was as good an operations manager as Roger had ever seen. He became Roger's right hand man. As theft problems were taken care of, and the overcharges for foam were a thing of the past, the operating statements were showing ever improving margins of profit.

Several weeks after they had moved in Evvy was hired by the South Carolina Department of Education as a Training Consultant for Special Education teaching personnel. The children were enrolled in a nearby combination elementary and middle school complex. Each of them was the only black child in their class. This did present some problems as making friends was difficult for them. They were making some progress and Evvy and Roger were pleased with the apparent assimilation of their families into what was essentially a white society. There had been no overt hostility shown to any member of the family,

The months flew by and it was approaching Thanksgiving Day and Roger priced out frozen turkeys at the nearby Bi-Lo Super market. There were 224 employees and at discount price of $12.50 each, it seemed like a great investment to provide a ticket to each employee to pick up a turkey at the local Bi-Lo in each area. In some cases Roger knew it would be a meal some of the families would enjoy only because of the company's gesture.

It proved very popular and paid dividends in increased productivity and employee morale. In addition the lawsuit against David Atkins and Ellwood Austin was being processed by Bryce, Hennings and Smith, Sperling's law firm in Charlotte, and it appeared that a trial date would be set sometime after Christmas.

Between both Evvy's and Roger's salaries they were saving over fifteen hundred dollars a month in addition to their IRAs. The family was happy and they enjoyed their affluence and status. Evvy loved her job and life was good. Roger was making the Sperling Mattress Company a major brand name in the area with new models, the addition of latex and memory foam mattresses and second day delivery. With additional sales came additional profits and for Isaac Newfeld life was also good. At the rate sales and profits were moving, Roger anticipated that he might earn almost a twenty thousand dollar bonus for the year. It seemed that his and Evvy's fear of race problems was nonexistent. Yes, life was good and getting better.

CHAPTER 11

For Roger and his family, life went from paradise to a nightmare on the morning of December 2nd. Roger was conducting a sales meeting with the eighteen sales representatives that Sperling South now employed. Roger had set up the meeting to introduce several new models that would go into production after the first of the year. The meeting was in the remodeled show room, and was going very well when Roger's cell phone rang. Daisy said, "I hate to interrupt you Mr. Maynard, but there are two gentlemen here from the Sheriff's office and they say they have to speak with you at once." Roger said to the group of sales reps., "Something has come up that I have to take care of, take a break. I'll be back shortly." Then into his cell phone he said, "Show them into my office, I'll be right there."

As Roger walked down the hall to his office, a wave of apprehension swept over him. He arrived at the doorway of his office just as Daisy and the two gentlemen did. One already had his badge and ID card out, identifying him as Deputy Bruce Hazelit, and by this point the other, younger man displayed similar identification as Deputy Mark Kearns. Roger stepped into his office and said, "How may I help you gentlemen?" Bruce Hazelit, the older of the two said, "You can help us by putting on your coat and coming with us to headquarters." Roger asked, "Am I under arrest?

Do you have a warrant?" The other Deputy said, "We'll ask the questions, now move." Deputy Hazelit said, "Yes, we do have a warrant for your arrest." as he unfolded a paper and held it up for Roger to read. He folded it up before Roger could read it. Roger put on his suit coat and top coat, and Deputy Kearns said, "Now put your hands out, Boy. I've got to cuff you."

Roger said, "Is this really necessary, I'm not going to try to escape or anything?" The Deputy said, "Boy, you better listen. I told you to put your hands out in front of you so I can cuff you. Now if you don't want to do it easy, we can do it the hard way, it's up to you." Roger decided there was no sense resisting so he held out his wrists, and for the first time in his life he was hand cuffed. The two deputies ushered him through the office area and to their car in the parking lot. Once in the car Roger asked again, "What is this all about? I've done nothing wrong." Deputy Hazelit said "You'all will get plenty of answers at the headquarters, so I advise you to shut up."

It was only a fifteen minute ride to the sheriff's office which was in the rear of the municipal building that also housed the Greenville Detention center, the morgue, and District courts.

Roger was escorted by the two deputies through what seemed to be a labyrinth of hallways to a room marked "Interrogations". The room was about twelve by twelve with a large mirror on one of the inside walls that Roger assumed was the viewing window from the other side. The walls were the same drab green paint as the hallways which gave the impression that it along with the rest of the building, wore out several decades ago. Roger's cuffs were removed and he was seated at a metal table which was fastened to the floor as was the straight back chair he was told to sit in. Then both deputies left, and locked the door to the room behind them.

After about a forty minute delay, the door opened and a large burly man with a neat gray beard entered the room. He introduced himself as Sheriff George Hardy, and took out a three by five file card and proceeded to read the Miranda Rights. When he finished, he placed the card and a pen in front of Roger, and instructed him to sign on the line acknowledging that his rights had been read to him and that he understood them. Roger signed and Sheriff Hardy collected the card and the pen and placed them in his inside coat pocket. He then ceremoniously removed his coat and placed it on the other chair back. He removed a small tape recorder from his belt and placing it on the table between them, he said, "You understand that this interrogation session will be recorded. The recorder is very sensitive so just speak in a normal voice. Roger said, "Fine, now can you tell me what this is all about?"

Sherriff Hardy replied "I would think you'd know, I mean you just don't murder a woman every day, or maybe you do." Roger said "I have no idea what the hell you are talking about. Hardy said "OK, it looks like we'll have to do this the long way. When did you last see Hanna Williams?" Roger said, "I am not answering any questions without an attorney present. I am invoking my right to remain silent." Sheriff Hardy said, "That's your right, but Son I can tell you it don't look good to lawyer up right from the git-go." Roger said, "I can't help that as I am not saying another word." Hardy shook his head and said, "Ok if that's the way you want it, fine."

He rose and pressed a button on the door frame and tilting his face toward a speaker grill over the door he spoke, "Come and get him, he lawyered up so you can take him to the lockup holding cell." Roger asked, "When do I get to contact an attorney or have someone contact one for me?" Hardy looked at his watch and said well it's just about lunch time now, and the switch board will not be back in operation for at least another hour or two." Roger said, "If you return my cell phone I won't have to trouble the switchboard personnel." Hardy shook his head and said, "Sorry, can't do that, rules are rules. Cell phones are a big no-no. By rights, I should take all your valuables, but we're friendly and since you'll only be in the holding cell for a few hours, we'll let you hold on to the rest of your stuff." At that moment Tweedle Dee and Tweedle Dum, the arresting deputies, appeared in the hallway, each taking an arm escorted Roger back through another labyrinth of hallways to the holding cell.

As the trio turned the corner and faced the bars of the holding cell, Roger froze in his tracks. Through the bars he saw Jamie Williams, the man he fired several months before and three other black men. Deputy Kearns pulled a key out of his pocket and unlocked the cell door, while Deputy Hazelit pushed Roger forward into the holding cell. Kearns closed the door and locked it. The two deputies turned and left the area at once.

Jamie Williams had a smile that was endless as he exclaimed, "Looky Heah, Looky Heah, It's da big boss man. Ahm gonna be a real gentleman and intro yo to mah friends heah. The really big dude stannin behind me is Big Ed Gordo, an the man holdin onto yo arm is Switch Johnson, an thet dude sittin on the bench is Eyes Quentin. This is the king of the mattress factry. Whacha do man to be in heah? Didja spit on the sidewalk? Yo fucka yo aint got much shit to say now that yo don have thet big fancy desk tween us. I tol yo thet somday I see yo outside. Yo is now wid some Brothahs an I'se owes yo somthang." With that Jamie Williams slashed across Rogers face with a vicious backhand. "I owes yo mo, but we'll git to that, but firss I want that fancy watch yo have on." Roger said, "Go to hell, that's a gift from my wife" Roger could feel a trickle of blood on his lip and the taste of blood in his mouth. Roger saw Ed Gordo's punch coming, but he could not avoid it and the blow caught him square in the face. There was darkness and the pain faded as he fell to the floor and lost consciousness.

CHAPTER 12

Roger heard a distant calling of his name. There was a hollow, almost echo like sound to the voice. He came to slowly with an increasing amount of pain as consciousness returned. His nose was the most painful spot along with his lips that were thick and swollen. He was laying on the bench and as he touched his face he could feel the encrusted blood around his mouth and nose. He started to sit up but he became so dizzy that he laid his head back. Sheriff Hardy slowly came into focus and he said, "Maynard it's 4:00 in the afternoon. If you want to reach your attorney, you better call soon or you'll miss him. We let you sleep as the boys that were in here said you weren't feeling well. They said you had stumbled and hit your head on the floor."

Roger looked around and saw that he was the only one in the holding cell. He sat up slowly and he asked, "Where are the guys that were in here?" Hardy replied, "They were locked up last night on a D & DP, disorderly and disturbing the peace, and they had a Magistrate hearing and were released after paying their fines." It was at that point that Roger noticed that his shoes were missing, as well as his top coat, watch, and pen. He checked his wallet and all of his cash was missing, about $225.00. Roger asked when he would be able to leave and Hardy said, "That's up to what your lawyer can work out with the District Court Judge and the Prosecutor's office. None of that happens until tomorrow morning." Roger said, "I'll call my wife and she can get in touch with the lawyer and she'll need to bring me some clean clothes and shoes." Hardy nodded and said, "It's your choice."

Roger was getting angrier by the second and as Hardy was turning to leave and lock the cell Roger exploded, "Hold it, Sheriff you and this city are not getting off this easy. I need medical attention and I am holding your office responsible for the loss of my money, shoes, watch, topcoat, and my suit if the blood stains don't come out. You arrest me and will not tell me what I am charged with, then throw me into a cell with a bunch of cut throat lowlifes who beat the hell out of me and robbed me. I assure you that you have not heard the end of this."

Sheriff Hardy scratched his head and said, "Well. I thought the deputies told you, you're charged with the murder of one Hanna Williams, that woman you've been runnin with on the side." Roger literally shouted, "That's totally ridiculous I haven't seen the woman since she showed up in my office about two months ago! I demand that you or one of your deputies take me over to Greenville Medical Center to be checked out. I believe I may have a concussion."

Hardy conceded, "Okay if you want medical attention that's what we'll get you." With that he closed and locked the cell door. About three minutes later Deputy Hazelit opened the cell and placed cuffs on Roger and said, "I'm taking you to the Doctor, Boy."

Roger said, "Knock off the "Boy" crap. It's demeaning and those comments are going to be part of my law suit against this city." There was no further conversation and after a twenty minute ride to the Emergency Room of the Greenville Medical Center, Roger saw a Doctor. He told the Doctor what had happened, and after an examination and clean up of his wounds, the Doctor said, "You have a broken nose, lacerations to your lips, several loose teeth and probably a slight concussion." The Doctor said, "Mr. Maynard, in view of the probable concussion we should keep you here for observation tonight." Deputy Hazelit who had been silent the entire time said, "Damn if I'm going to stay here all night to guard him." "Well medically a concussion can be very serious and could even cause death. He needs to be monitored at least for the next ten or twelve hours", the Doctor retorted.

Deputy Hazelit cuffed Roger to the examining table and stepped out to call Sheriff Hardy.

When he returned he said, "The Sheriff says it's OK to keep him overnight. I'll be with him until midnight and then Kearns will be here overnight til 8:00 AM. A little overtime pay helps with Christmas coming and all."

Roger borrowed the Doctor's cell phone and called Evvy. She could not believe the story he told, and that was with him leaving out some of the uglier details. She brought him clean clothes, shoes, some cash, shaving gear, and her cell phone. Roger called Newfeld and explained what had happened, and that he had no idea how he had been connected to a murdered woman and charged with her murder. Newfeld said that he would call the corporate law firm and have them get an affiliate in the Greenville area to be at the courthouse in the morning. Issac wished him luck and told him that whatever the bail or bond financial arrangement, the company would back it. Finally Evvy left to get back home to the kids and Roger with one hand cuffed to the bed rail fell into a deep and troubled sleep. He slept fitfully until midnight when he was awakened by the voices of Deputy Hazelit and Kearns.

Roger finally got back to sleep and woke with a start as Deputy Kearns was unlocking the cuffs. He told Roger to shower, shave and dress, they were due in Court in an hour and a half. Roger stood up next to the bed and almost fell over as he was light headed and he had a headache that was like none he had ever experienced before. He staggered into the bath room and looked in the mirror. His nose was swollen and his lips were puffy and bruised looking. Even with his darker skin, he could see the precursor of twin black eyes. After shaving and showering, he felt a little better, but was definitely feeling the effect of the beating he sustained.

Deputy Kearns said, "We have a few minutes to kill so do you feel up to a quick cup of coffee, courtesy of the City of Greenville." Roger said, "Ok but I need to have the doctor sign me out. This turned out to be a half hour process as it took ten minutes for a doctor to show up and another ten minutes for the examinations and filling out paperwork, and finally ten more minutes for an orderly to bring a wheelchair to roll him out to the pickup area. While Kearns got the car Roger was handcuffed to a wrought iron railing.

CHAPTER 13

They bought coffee at a kiosk in the lobby of the courthouse. A well dressed gentleman approached them and asked if one of them was Roger Maynard. Roger answered in the affirmative. The man introduced himself as Thomas Hennings of Bryce, Hennings and Smith, and said that he was assigned to cover Roger's bail hearing, and that his firm is affiliated with Newfeld's attorneys in New York.

Hennings had a guard place them in one of the attorney/client conference rooms and Deputy Kearns removed the cuffs and remained outside the door. Hennings said, "Mr.

Maynard, you are charged with first degree murder of a woman, who according to the charging documents, was your mistress. How will you plead?" Roger replied, "Not Guilty of course. I know this is some kind of frame-up, as I have made a number of people very angry since I took over management of the plant." Hennings responded, "I doubt that we will get into that at this hearing. The prosecution will want to deny bail, but we'll argue that your release poses no threat to the public, that you do not present a flight risk, and try to obtain your release on a bond." Roger said, "It's probably obvious from my appearance that I have been severely physically abused. The sheriffs' people put me into a holding cell with some hardened criminals, without any oversight and I was beaten to unconscious by four thugs, one of whom I fired at the plant several months ago. They also stole my shoes, an expensive watch, my top coat and about $ 225.00 I had in my wallet. What are we going to do about that? I want to sue them for valuables taken and also punitive damages for my suffering." Hennings replied that, "Was a totally different issue and not one to be brought up at this hearing."

The hearing was scheduled for 10:45 AM before a Judge Anthony Mellor. Hennings gave a formidable performance in fighting the prosecution's request for incarceration until trial and finally managed to get Judge Mellor to set the bond at $ 250,000. The prosecutor, Bruce Andrews, argued that the murder of Hanna William was vicious and more brutal than any previous murder in Greenville. Fortunately, Hennings prevailed and told the court he was fully authorized to handle the bond arrangements.

After Judge Mellor's ruling, Roger asked Hennings if he would handle his defense. Hennings told him, "I'm sorry Mr. Maynard, but I think you would be better served to find a good criminal attorney as neither I, nor my firm handle criminal cases. We specialize in corporate legal work. I hope you understand and I wish you every success in proving your innocence." He asked Hennings if he could recommend a good defense lawyer and Hennings said he would look into it and call Roger. Roger called Evvy and informed her that he was free on bond, and that he would see her that evening. Next he called Frank at the plant and asked Frank to pick him up at the courthouse. While Roger was waiting, he purchased a paper in the coffee shop. He found his name in the blaring headlines and a picture of himself taken unbeknownst to him as the deputies ushered him into the sheriff's office.

Frank picked him up as requested and said, “Roger you have made some powerful enemies since you took over. I have a feeling that you have been setup.”

Roger said, “There is no question about it as I know I am innocent.” Frank said, “Oh, Mr. Newfeld called and said he is flying in tomorrow morning to see you. Roger groaned, “Oh my, he’s just about the last person I need to see right now.” Roger spent a short afternoon in the office as he had many things to do and he wanted to get home, Besides, his head was still throbbing.

Evvy came home early and Roger kissed her and said, “Evvy I want you to know that I am completely innocent of that woman’s murder, and more importantly, that I have been totally faithful to you since the day we met. I never had any kind of affair going on with this Hanna Williams as the paper implies.” Evvy told him, “I believe you and you have my complete support. I noticed a chill in the air in my office and not one of my white colleagues asked or mentioned anything about the story in the morning paper. Damn, I think anything derogatory about a black person, that is said or printed, is believed until it is proved otherwise.”

“Before I’m finished, I am going to prove this was all a set up”, Roger replied.

Evvy said, “The kids are due home anytime now, I wonder if they know what is going on?”

Within a few minutes, Davon’s school bus dropped him at the corner and he ran into the house waving a paper which he said was his house. Roger took it from him and it really did resemble their home. Roger said “good job Davey, you even got the red shutters on the windows. Great picture.”

At that point Lola came through the door crying, “The kids are saying that Dad is a killer and they don’t want a killer’s kids in their school. It started at recess and they chanted "killer's kid" most of the bus ride home. I don't want to go back to that school." Between sobs, she asked, "What is going on? Oh Daddy what happened to you? You look like you've been in an accident."

Roger thought for a moment before answering her, and as usual, the truth in Rogers mind was always the correct answer. He said, "Well, the truth is that some very bad men beat Daddy while he was arrested. You're going to hear a lot of nasty things about your me, but they are all lies. I have not done anything wrong. You have got to believe that and not let others make you feel bad. Your Mom and I haven't discussed it, but it may be advisable to allow you and your brother to stay home for a few days."

Evvy who was sitting on the sofa with tears in her eyes, said, "I think that would be a very good idea. I'm going into my office tomorrow and try to take a few days off myself. You know Roger, I think it would probably be best if you stayed home for a few days also." Roger said, "No, I can't because Issac is flying in tomorrow. I guess Newfeld wants to see firsthand what is going on."

With that thought in mind, Roger called the New York office to see what time Newfeld's flight would arrive. Newfeld's secretary gave Roger the flight information and that he was scheduled to land at 10:55 am. Roger said that he would meet him. Roger was not looking forward to seeing Isaac under these circumstances. The rest of the day went quietly as the kids seemed to settle into their usual routines with Lola reading and Davey playing with his legos. Evvy fixed an early dinner and afterward they spent some time with the children and watched TV. The kids had their regular bedtime at nine and at ten the news came on out of Charlotte.

The local portion quickly turned to the *Brutal murder of a Greenville woman named Hanna Williams.* The anchor then elaborated that, "The woman had been found early this morning behind a motel. She had been stabbed sixteen times and left for dead in back of a trash bin. Police said that they have arrested a suspect, who is now free on bond. The Greenville sheriff's office said that no weapon has been found and the motive is under investigation. The suspect in the killing is a prominent business man who just recently moved to Greenville to run a mattress factory for the new owners. His name is Roger Maynard and he is a resident of Glenwood Commons in suburban Greenville." With this, they flashed a picture of Roger which was the publicity photo that was sent to the local media when the Sperling Mattress Co. announced the buyout, and Roger's appointment to head the new division. The news then went on to a story about a local youth who drowned in lake near Charlotte.

Shortly thereafter Roger and Evvy turned off the TV and the lights and retired to the bedroom. Roger had Evvy take some close up photos of his injuries while they were still reasonably fresh. Although Roger had the hospital examination as evidence, he felt it would not hurt to have the pictures. Roger was in the bathroom when he heard the phone ring. Evvy answered it and after she announced Maynard residence, a voice said, "Why don't you high faluting niggers go the hell back to where you come from. We don't need any more nigger murderers here. If you all know what's good for you, you all git out real quick." Evvy said, "Who is this? Give me your name." The caller replied, "Ain't no need to know, jus know what's good for you and git." With that the caller hung up.

As Roger walked into the bedroom he started to ask, "who was calling this....." His words trailed off as he saw

Evvy sitting on the side of the bed sobbing with the phone still in her hand. Between sobs she repeated the caller's words and then said, "If I could, I would pack up the kids and you and I in the car and hit 85 north right now."

Roger took the phone from her hand and sat down next to her on the side of the bed. He put his arm around her and said "Honey, where is that fighter who has often kept me in the battle? We can't let this defeat us, and I'm not going to give in to a bunch of bigots and thugs. You can't either."

Evvy said, "How could you ever get involved with this woman in the first place, I just don't understand."

Roger said, "Baby, I was not involved in any way with this woman. When I get my day in court it will be obvious that this was a complete frame up. I only spoke to this woman on two occasions, once in a restaurant and once in my office. I never had any relations with this woman, and that is not a Bill Clinton type of denial. It is the truth. I'm so sorry Evvy, if you're thinking that I was in any way unfaithful to you. It did not, and never would happen, I love you so much."

Evvy said, "I'm sorry if I had any doubt." They kissed and finished getting ready for bed. Their sleep was restless and troubled.

CHAPTER 14

The next morning Roger picked up Isaac Newfeld at the airport. It was near noon by the time his flight landed. As Roger waited in the gate area, a woman said to the man she was with, "Honey, look, I think it's that murderer whose picture was in the paper yesterday."

The man nodded in agreement and they quickly moved across to the other side of the gate area. Finally Isaac came through the gate with a scowl on his face as he hated delays on public transportation. He felt it wasted his time. Roger could tell he was clearly in a bad mood.

"Roger, Roger, What is going on? What happened to your face?" These were the first words out of Isaac's mouth. Roger said hello to Isaac and shook his hand and asked if he could help him with his piece of luggage or briefcase. Isaac handed Roger his carryon bag. Roger led the way out of the Greenville airport and to his car. They did not speak until they were in Roger's car.

Roger said, "It's not complicated, I have been framed. By whom, I don't know. I have stepped on the toes of the previous foam supplier and as you know I am working with our attorneys in New York to sue him. Also, I have done some house cleaning in the plants and in the process fired a man who may be part of a local mob family. In addition one man I fired was in the holding cell they threw me into.

He and his friends worked my face over and stole from me while I was unconscious. That is what is going on."

Isaac said, "Well, let's discuss it after we look at the plant." Shortly they were at the plant and Roger introduced Isaac to Frank and the three of them went through all of the plant operations. Isaac was very pleased and he complimented Roger and Frank on the increase in production efficiency as it was showing up on the bottom line. By that point it was early afternoon and Isaac took Roger and Frank to lunch, and the conversation was completely about the business. After they returned to the plant, Frank left them and Roger and Isaac went into his office.

Roger closed the door and asked Isaac what he wanted to know. Isaac said, "What I want to know is how in the hell did you get mixed up with this woman who was killed?" Roger told him of his two encounters with Hanna Williams, of meeting her in a restaurant and a second time when she called on him as a salesperson for the previous foam supplier. He also told Isaac of the time she visited the motel he stayed in prior to moving down, and wanted to visit him in the late evening. Roger finished his summary and said, "That is the extent of my very distant involvement with this woman."

Isaac shook his head and said, "What is it with you people that somehow trouble always finds you."

Roger stood up and said, "You people!, You People!, you mean Blacks, Negroes? Don't you? Isaac you are the last person in the world I thought would be prejudiced. Didn't Hitler say "you people" are the cause of all our problems, meaning Jews? I am tired of bigoted remarks and innuendoes. I have worked my ass off getting through college and earning an MBA, and I have many times sacrificed personal events with my family to make Sperling Mattress a success. I'm tired of it, I feel like an innocent bystander who has been splattered with mud and labeled a murderer. This is affecting Evvy and my kids, so don't sit there and intimate in any way that this is my fault. If you want to fire me go ahead, I'll fight this on my own."

"Roger, Roger, don't get upset. I meant nothing by my remark. I just meant that,... well, it doesn't matter. I don't want to fire you and I want you to know you have the full financial support of the company and me personally. I spoke with Mr. Hennings about defending you and he said that his firm couldn't get involved as they have many corporate clients here and that they would not take kindly to the firm defending a black. I know that the level of prejudice is just below the surface down here, my youngest son went to the University of Georgia for two years, and he gave up as he couldn't take it. Just hang in there Roger, I know it will work out, and take off whatever time you need for your defense."

Roger held out his hand and said, "I apologize for the blow up, but I have had this subtle race issue up to my ears. I am tired of it, I will assume you meant nothing by your comment. My next important step is to find a good defense lawyer who has no qualms about defending a black man."

Isaac said, "Find a good Jewish lawyer as they are generally very enthusiastic about getting into a case that involves prejudice. Jewish attorneys in New York fought each other for a chance to represent the Rosenbergs in their spy trial."

Roger looked up the local bar association members on the internet and found only 3 attorneys in the Greenville/ Spartanburg area, and they were all just in practice for several years. He widened his search to Atlanta and found several who seemed to be seasoned attorneys. He checked out their records and found one who had been involved in several civil rights cases and had a winning record. Roger called the office of Rueben Jackman and found that his fee was $ 400.00 per hour with the time starting when he left his Atlanta office, and running until he was back. In addition they pointed out that he would probably incur rental of a private plane or air fare, a rental car, and hotel room when he arrived and of course meals, it would also include secretarial time and research assistants. Roger reviewed the cost with Isaac, and Newfeld said, "Don't worry about it just send his bills to my office and I will have them paid."

Isaac stayed over and turned down Roger's offer to put him up in his home, instead spending the night at the Greenville Hilton. The next morning Roger picked him up at the hotel and took him to the airport for his early flight. As Isaac got out of Roger's car, he leaned across the seat, shook Rogers' hand wished him well and said, "You know Roger that remark I made yesterday, I did mean blacks. I'm glad you called me on it because sometimes these kind of thoughts just become a part of one's thinking, and it obviously happened. All I can say is I'm sorry and it won't happen again. My God, I don't even think of you as black or any other race, just a very bright fellow human. Again, my sincere apologies." Roger said, "Thanks, your honesty means a great deal to me. Have a safe trip home, and call me tomorrow, I am going to Atlanta and I'll let you know if Mr. Rueben Jackman, Esquire, will represent me or not."

CHAPTER 15

Things were relatively quiet at the plant and it seemed that everyone steered clear of Roger except for Frank. Roger briefed Frank on his plan to go to Atlanta the following day and they reviewed schedules, and made plans for Frank to take over complete control of all operations until Roger was rid of the Albatross which these accusations had become. That evening he told Evvy of his plans and discussed his meeting with Isaac. Evvy seemed somewhat relieved that Roger had a definite plan and not just the bravado of a man with his back against a wall, The kids had stayed home from school and Evvy also obtained permission to take off a few days. It seemed as though life was returning to some semblance of order in the Maynard household.

A short while after dinner, the chimes announced that someone was at their door. Roger was drying pots and pans, and Evvy was packing the dishwasher. Lola went to the door. Roger and Evvy listened but could only hear a low murmur of voices. Evvy dried her hands and stepped into the living room. Lola had ushered in two elderly women, who Evvy recognized at once. They were the Radcliffe sisters, Simpson and Anna, neighbors who lived on the other side of the Ward's house. Mrs. Ward had told Evvy about them one day as Mrs. Ward tended her garden. They were in their seventies and had inherited the home from their Father.

Neither had ever been married and as Mrs. Ward put it "they were the do-gooders of the neighborhood, with fixing meals for sick neighbors on the block, sending get well cards, and otherwise just being good neighbors."

They introduced themselves and Anna, the older of the two said, "We have never talked to black people before, other than to give instructions to people who came to do work for us. So please forgive us if we say something wrong or something we shouldn't say." Roger had come in from the kitchen and Evvy introduced him and Lola to the sisters, Davey was in the basement playing. Simpson Radcliffe said, "Mr. Maynard, we just wanted to say hello and that we are sorry for the pain you and your family must be going through. We see you come home every evening and you seem like a good family man. Actually all of you seem like a good family, maybe like that family that Mr. Cosby had on TV. Anyway we just wanted to say if you need any character witnesses when your trial starts we'll be glad to testify for you." Simpson spoke up and said, "We only know black people from what we watch on TV. Are you funny like that "Flip Wilson" man, or Mr. Cosby?"

Roger said, "Thank you for your concerns. My family and I are honored to have met you and for your thoughtfulness, and unfortunately I don't think I could be compared to Flip Wilson, or Bill Cosby. Evvy made a great coconut custard pie for desert, why don't you join us for a slice of pie and a cup of coffee or tea?"

Anna begged off for her sister and herself as she said, "We never miss Wheel of Fortune since we like that young Pat Sajac, but we think that woman on the show should wear dresses that a proper woman would wear, not those flimsy things." Evvy and Roger again thanked them for coming by and their concern. After they left Roger said, "If everyone was like our neighbors I would not worry about the charges against me. It gives me faith in the human race, at least the ones who live here on our street."

Tomorrow was a crucial day for Roger so they turned in early as Roger had a two and a half hour drive to Atlanta and his eleven o'clock appointment with the legendary Rueben Jackman, Esquire. A meeting that could shape Roger's future for better or worse.

Chapter 16

Roger made good time driving down to Atlanta. The traffic on I85 was light until he hit the outskirts of the city, then it slowed to a crawl. His GPS unit took him to the address on Peach Tree street. It was a modern glass and stone office building with Mr. Jackman holding court in offices on the seventeenth floor. Roger entered a rather opulent entry foyer and went to the reception desk. He gave an attractive, young oriental girl his name and stated that he had an appointment with Mr. Jackman. She picked up a phone and said something that Roger could not hear, and then came around the reception desk and asked him to follow her.

The carpet on the floors was plush and you could feel each step sink into it, and the furnishings were expensive and in good taste. They stopped in front of an office and she opened the door and announced that Mr. Roger Maynard was here for his appointment. A handsome young man said, "Please have a seat Mr. Maynard, I'll be with you in a moment. Can I have them bring you a coffee or tea?

Roger said, "My appointment was with Mr. Jackman, what goes?"

"My name is Phil Spiegel and I do initial interviews for Mr. Jackman. He's a very busy man and I gather all the facts of a potential case so that he can evaluate them quickly and determine if he wishes to represent you. Now shall we get started with you relating the facts of your arrest and truthful involvement in this matter.?

Roger could not contain himself. "Look dammit, I drove all the way down here from Greenville for this meeting and I was led to believe that I would speak with Mr. Jackman. If he can't take thirty or forty minutes to speak with me, you can shove it, I'm a busy man also."

"Now, now, Mr. Maynard, this is standard procedure in our office, as Mr. Jackman simply does not have the time to speak to every person who would want his representation. Would you want him to take his time and attention away from your case just to spend time on something that he will end up ditching.?"

Roger said, "No I don't suppose I would. Well if this step is necessary, let's get to it and get it over with so that God can decide whether or not he wishes to represent me."

Phil Spiegel said, "Mr. Maynard, may I call you Roger?" Roger answered affirmatively. Spiegel went on to say, "Well fine, let's start with your arrest and take it from there until you were released on bond." Roger told of the Deputies visit to his office, their biased attitude and calling him Boy. He then described his encounter with Sheriff Hardy, his beating and robbery in the holding cell, his treatment at the hospital, and he brought a copy of the Greenville Courier with its front page splash of the murder, featuring a pictures of Roger and Hanna Williams.

Spiegel then asked Roger to be as truthful as he can be, to the best of his knowledge in describing his contacts and involvement with Hanna Williams. He said, "I need to have every intimate detail, I am not here to judge, but just to get all of the facts and details that may impinge on the case." Roger summarized his brief contacts with Hanna and said,

"That is the entire truth. Now let me tell you my theory of who may be trying to frame me."

He proceeded to describe, "The sour relationship with David Atkins, the owner of Great International Foam Corporation, who Sperling is getting ready to sue for fraud, gross overcharges and sub quality materials. In addition I fired a man at the plant for theft, and rumor has it that his family is somehow involved with the local Mafia. Whether they could be involved in this frame-up, I don't know. What is definite, is that someone has set me up."

After reviewing Roger's personal history, it seemed that Phil Spiegel had run out of questions and topics. Roger said, "Mr. Spiegel what's your opinion, do you think Mr, Jackman will want to take this case?"

Phil leaned back in his chair and said, "I am almost certain he will take the case it has all of the elements that he looks for. Overt prejudice by public officials, an uncaring approach to your safety by officials, the possibility of a frame-up, a civil suit against the City of Greenville, plus your very lack of any personal involvement with this woman. Yes, I think this is a case that's made to order for Rueben."

Roger asked, "When will I know for sure?" Phil answered, "Within forty-eight hours." They shook hands and Roger said, "I apologize for my attitude a little earlier, but I'm sure you understand, it's my life and the future of my family, I was disappointed that I didn't get to speak with him." Phil said, "I understand. I'll get back to you as soon as I can review this with Rueben. Thank you for coming in." So ended Roger's Atlanta meeting with some confidence, but the thread of uncertainty was still dangling in the breeze.

CHAPTER 17

Roger drove back to Greenville disappointed as he still did not have definite representation. He called Evvy and told her about the meeting and that he was frustrated. Evvy seemed depressed on the phone and Roger could think of nothing to say that would brighten her mood. He told her that he was going into his office for a few hours, and that he would be home about five pm.

There was a message waiting for him to call Newfeld, which he did first thing. Isaac just wanted to know how the meeting went. Roger summarized it and there being nothing new to discuss they said "so long." Frank tapped on the door frame of Roger's office and said, "Do you have a few minutes?" Roger said yes and Frank came in and closed the door behind him. "I have some information that may be of interest and I hope may be helpful to your case. Yesterday at lunch time, I overheard a couple of our sewing department employees talking about the murder. It seems that several of the ladies know Jamie Williams rather well and they were saying that Hanna Williams is his older sister. In addition, the ladies said Jamie did not get along with Hanna as he often tried to bum money or borrow her car from her to no avail. One lady who lives near Jamie said she heard that they had a big fight over money the week before the murder."

Roger asked, "Can you document the date, time, names of the ladies, and who said what? This could be an important bit of information. Thanks Frank, I really appreciate it. If you hear anything else keep me posted."

Shortly after Frank left his office, the phone rang, and Daisy announced that a Mr. Jackman was on line two. Roger thanked her and pressed the flashing button and said, "Roger Maynard here." A deep baritone voice said, "Hello, this Rueben Jackman and I have reviewed your case with great interest. I am definitely going to represent you. Can you drive down the day after tomorrow, and spend several hours with me? I will have what discovery items the State has by tomorrow, there will probably be more as they continue their investigation, but this will give us some idea of where they are heading." Roger responded, "Of course Mr. Jackman. What would be a good time for you?" Jackman said, "Please call me Rueben, and about one o'clock would work for me." With that they ended their conversation.

Roger was elated, He called Evvy and gave her the good news, then he call Isaac Newfeld, who told Roger that he had Jackman checked out, and that he is one of the best in the country. Isaac said he would have a letter sent via overnight courier stating that the company assumes all liability for all charges, fees, miscellaneous costs, etc., along with a check for $10,000.00, Mr. Jackman's normal retainer. Roger thanked Isaac and promised to keep him posted.

Roger could hardly wait for his appointment with Rueben. He hadn't experienced such a feeling of anticipation since he was a child waiting for Christmas morning. The following day passed slowly as Roger tried to involve himself in busy work at the office. Things were running smoothly and he found it difficult to concentrate on the business. Frank was an excellent plant manager and seldom did he find it necessary to involve Roger in the day to day operations. The only significant happening was an altercation between two of the ladies from the sewing department in the cafeteria area. Frank had stepped in and defused the argument before it became physical.

At home Evvy had gone back to work and the kids were back in school, it seemed as if the entire arrest experience was just a bad dream. A sudden tidal wave on a surface of gentle ripples. Roger knew that Evvy was very worried. She went about her household chores as if she was sleep walking. She was moody, and hardly watched television and although she was a voracious reader, she took no interest in what was normally her favorite pastime. Even Lola and Davey seemed more subdued than normal. All these subtle signs reminded Roger that the nightmare was far from over.

CHAPTER 18

Roger was early for his appointment with Reuben Jackman. As he waited, he stood at one of the reception room windows and watched the vehicle and pedestrian traffic seventeen floors below. It was an impressive view of downtown Atlanta. He mused that perhaps after this mess was over with, he should look into upgrading his career with a Fortune 500 company where there would be more opportunities to move up. Realistically, he was at a dead end in his present employment. Unless Isaac decided to sell the business to some large conglomerate, all he could expect is moderate annual increases and the same responsibilities, unless he was able to expand the Southern Division.

At that moment he heard the receptionist saying, "Mr. Maynard, Mr. Jackman will see you now." As he turned away from the window, the receptionist was approaching him and asked him to follow her. Rueben occupied a large corner office with windows on two walls. The room was very tastefully furnished in earth-tones with accents of blue. Roger was surprised when Rueben walked around his desk to shake hands. For some reason Roger had visualized Rueben as a large man. Instead Rueben was thin and about five foot three, with black hair, glasses, and a small goatee.

They shook hands and Rueben motioned Roger to sit in one of the occasional chairs facing the sofa. Rueben took the chair to Roger's right. He held a file folder and an Apple notebook. They engaged in some "get acquainted, break the ice type of small talk" for several minutes and finally Rueben said, "Shall we get started." Roger said yes and asked if the prosecutor's office had sent him what they had on discovery. Rueben said they had and he opened the folder.

"Well Roger, what they have is pretty much a circumstantial case; however, in spite of what you told Phil Spiegel, they do have a DVD of you and Hanna having sex in what is obviously a motel room. That is their most damaging piece of evidence. Before we get to that lets review the other evidence."

Roger said in an astonished voice, "A DVD of me having sex with Hanna Williams. Impossible!! To quote an ex-president, I never had sex with that woman."

Rueben said, "I had my electronic expert review the DVD and he says it has been very heavily edited. We never see Hanna's face only her nude body and only from the back. The angle of the camera suggests that the camera was hidden in a ceiling heat or air vent toward the front of the room, so as to give a full image of the bed."

Roger asked, "Could we view the DVD as if it is what I think, it could clear-up most of the questions pertaining to my relationship with the murdered woman.

Rueben said, "I would prefer to follow the discovery in order, but if you feel it would save time, let's take a look."

Ruben slipped the DVD into his laptop and in seconds, a somewhat grainy picture appeared on the screen. Roger stood to the side of Jackman's chair so that he could view the DVD. Rueben clicked on the play icon and the image became sharper with the movements of a man and woman embracing, kissing and then removing each other's clothing. There is a break and the next images are a man and woman nude on the bed with the woman astride Roger so that her face is not visible. Roger said, "Stop it!", and Rueben pressed a button and the image froze. Roger then asked if Rueben could zoom in on the woman's back, Ruben answered in the affirmative. As the woman's back became larger Roger exclaimed, "There it is, see the small rose tattoo on her left hip?" Roger said,

"That's my wife. When she was down to see the home I selected, we went to the motel and engaged in sex, sort of a pent up thing on both our parts as being down here a week or two at a time by myself is not conducive to a satisfying sex life. They must have had a proximity switch installed somewhere near the door which activated the camera when it sensed the mass of two people. It's known as a capacitance sensor. Ask your electronic expert about it, we use them in certain conveyor applications in the Newark plant.

Evvy and Hanna are almost the same size, and they have identical skin coloration. When whoever is behind this effort to frame me, saw this, they decided that they would carefully edit out the woman's face in this video and say it was Hanna. Maybe you can talk to the Prosecutor's office and have them drop this entire ridiculous witch hunt with me and concentrate on finding woman's real killer."

Rueben shook his head, and said, "No, no, you don't want that. Such a thing would be buried in a one column by two inch deep blurp on page twenty of the paper, if it's printed at all. What will be remembered by the community is the front page story, pictures and headlines. A trial by Jury where you will be acquitted of all charges is what you want. That is what will be a front page story. It will also help with the civil trial for damages which I will pursue for you after the acquittal. This would be a so called "sensation trial" with a successful, well educated Afro-American involved in a sultry affair with a "sometime prostitute" who is found murdered. It will be the front-page story for however many days the trial continues. I want to show the prosecution and the sheriff's office to be inept, prejudiced. and lazy. Believe me, it will make your civil suit go like a breeze. I think we can walk away with a huge monetary award and public apologies."

Roger considered what Rueben told him for a few moments, and said, "If you think this is our best path, let's go for it." As Rueben outlined the other evidence, Roger tried to respond to each allegation. First was the meeting with Hanna in the restaurant while Roger was having dinner. Roger responded that he invited her to sit at his table, as he was anxious to learn all he could about the area, as quickly as possible. He wished to have a better knowledge of schools and housing areas since these were important aspects for his family. He told Rueben it was just a conversation at the end of which she virtually offered herself but he solidly declined.

As Rueben flipped papers going through the file folder, he asked Roger about her visit to his office at the plant. Roger said, "She came to our offices posing as a vendor's sales representative. Whether or not this was true, I have no idea, My office door was open the entire duration of her visit which was probably less than five minutes. I dismissed dealing with her company as I had previously accused her employer of fraudulent practices, and that my company is pursuing a law suit against its owner, Mr. Dave Atkins. At that time she also invited me to dinner as she said she had an expense account. I declined, telling her that it was totally inappropriate."

Rueben then read from a paper which purported that she visited him in his motel room that same evening, and the prosecution said the sheriff's investigator had the testimony of the night room clerk, one George Simpson, who said he remembered Hanna coming in around eleven PM asking for Mr. Maynard's room number.

Roger responded, "That's pure unadulterated bullshit. The clerk called me and asked if I was receiving visitors, I said I wanted no visitors, and told him to tell Ms. Williams that if she needs to contact me, to try my office during regular business hours."

Rueben said, "Here's another investigator's report, they found her car yesterday parked on a business parking lot on a service road off of I85. They believe that she was murdered in her car as there is a great deal of blood residue in the car and that it is her blood."

Roger interjected, "Did they check for prints, I can tell you if they found any, they were not mine as I was never even near her car?"

Rueben replied, "According to the rest of the report, the steering wheel seemed to be wiped clean although there were some traces of blood on the wheel. The driver side door had some prints of one James Williams, the victim's brother. He was questioned and explained he had borrowed her car a week earlier to drive to Chesney as he had heard a mill there was hiring and he applied for a job." The potential employer "South River Textiles" was checked and did show that Mr. Williams had made an application for employment. With that verification any further investigation into James Williams was dropped"

Roger then told Rueben of the remarks from some of the sewing department ladies indicating that there was a very stormy relationship between Jamie and his older sister. Roger reached in his briefcase and gave Ruben, Frank's report with the names and addresses of the ladies in the sewing department who had voiced knowledge of bad blood between James Williams and Hanna Williams. Rueben said this would be extremely helpful for his investigator to follow up.

That seemed to be the sum and substance of the discovery evidence filed by the prosecutor's office. Rueben said, "I have every confidence that I will have you not only found just not guilty of the charges, but every charge completely dismissed due to flawed evidence, and total incompetence and/or bigotry. You will be a completely free man and in many eyes, the victim of a very biased system. In addition, we have two excellent possibilities for an SODDI defense, if we should need it, but I am certain we won't."

Roger looked puzzled and asked, "SODDI?".

Rueben smiled and said, "It stands for "Some Other Dude Did It." He chuckled and said, "If the Judge doesn't grant my motion for dismissal of all charges, there will be so much flawed evidence that even a jury of Klan members would find for acquittal of all charges."

Rueben said there were some aspects that he would have his investigator look into to see if there was any connection between a frame up by Atkins or if her brother Jamie murdered her. With that the meeting had drawn to a close and Rueben said, "I'm proud that you have selected me as there is evidence of racial persecution present here, and it's my goal to put a spotlight on it and stop it in its tracks. I'll be in touch to keep you up to date. Be happy, sleep well, and don't worry." Smiling Rueben continued, "Tell your Wife that things will be better than ever in just a few months after the trial takes place, so be happy, don't worry." With that Rueben held out his hand which Roger shook and they parted.

Roger retrieved his car from a nearby parking garage and before he even started his trip back up to Greenville, he called Evvy to give her a summary of the meeting which he felt would give her morale a much needed boost. She seemed enthusiastic about the report and even asked a few questions. Roger drove home much happier and confident than he was on his trip to Atlanta earlier in the day.

CHAPTER 19

The next several weeks flew by and it was Christmas. The year had been good for Sperling Mattress and Isaac had approved twenty-five dollar to one hundred dollar bonuses for all of the Southern Division employees. This had never happened before and employee morale was at an all time high. For many of the plant employees it meant the difference between a barren holiday and the ability to at least make their children happy. For the plant managers, it meant the ability to buy their wife a nice gift or give their family a debt free Christmas. Roger saw to it that Frank got a check for a thousand dollars. Frank was so appreciative that he had tears in his eyes thanking Rogers.

The plant closed for the week between Christmas and New Year, and it was a time for taking inventory, doing much needed maintenance on the equipment, and doing a hundred other things that are impossible to do while a plant is running. Roger went in most days, although they were short days, no seven or eight o'clock evenings as was often the case during normal operations. Evvy had to work several days that week and she came home in the late afternoon very depressed, as she felt ostracized by her coworkers. She said they spoke to her only as necessary for their mission, and crowded the lunch table so that she had taken to eating alone in her office.

Roger was deeply worried about Evvy as it seemed there was no amount of good news that could cheer her, and her depression was becoming noticeably more pronounced. Even the Christmas holiday failed to change her mood. With the children, it was always the happiest time of the year for Evvy. Fortunately, things had settled down for the kids as first graders didn't have a clue and sixth graders seemed to have very transient memories. Lola was happy as there was no more taunting or even a mention of her Father's problems. The newspaper and local TV news had no more reports other than a brief mention that Ms. Williams' car had been found and was obviously the murder scene. It seemed as though everyone involved had their proverbial fifteen minutes of fame, and life moved on.

Roger asked Frank if he could recommend a physician or therapist, as he felt that Evvy had reached the point of needing professional help. Frank recommended a GP that he and his wife went to and a therapist who helped him with depression after he gave up drinking. Roger called each one, only to find that the GP said outright he did not treat Blacks, and the Therapist after learning that Roger and his Wife were black said he was filled up with patients, and not taking on any new patients at that time, call back later. Roger called Jackman to see if he had any recommendations. He did, but the Psychiatrist was in the Atlanta area. None the less Roger made an appointment and he took off to drive Evvy down to Atlanta.

It was a tense trip as Evvy really saw no need for treatment, and resented that Roger made the appointment anyway. She slept most of the two and a half hour trip and hardly said five words to Roger, Fortunately, the Doctor's office was on the northeast side of Atlanta and they were able to avoid the downtown traffic. The Psychiatrist was a Doctor Reginald Sawyer and much to Rogers surprise he was black and at the most thirty-five.

Chapter 20

There was no one in the waiting room only a small laptop with instructions to sign in. Roger had no more than finished filling in the required information for Evvy when Dr. Sawyer stepped into the waiting room and informed Roger and Evvy that they were next and to follow him. They followed him down a hallway to an open door which was his office. He asked that they take a seat on a sofa and start by telling him why they were there.

Roger asked Evvy if she wanted to tell the Doctor why they were there, but she said, "You tell him, this was your idea, not mine." Roger said, "Very well, but first, I would like to introduce ourselves". Dr. Sawyer said, "That would be a good start, and when you finish, I'll tell you about me, then we'll all be on the same page." Roger proceeded to give quick summary of their marriage, education, present employment, and his current legal situation which he felt had precipitated Evvy's depression.

When Roger finished, Dr. Sawyer said, "I was born and raised in Chicago. Took my medical training at North Western and interned at John Hopkins Psychiatric Center in Baltimore. In case you're wondering why a black man from the north is settled in Georgia, it's because when I was in the Army, I was stationed at Camp Gordon, here in Georgia, I met my wife, a real Atlanta peach, and she didn't want to move away from her folks who are up in years and poor health. Now Evvy, if I may call you Evvy, I would like you to tell me if you think you are depressed, and if so what do you think is the reason?"

Evvy responded, "Well, Reggie if I may call you that, I don't think I'm suffering from depression. This entire situation that Roger finds himself in has just brought to mind how fleeting and fragile what we call happiness can be. I have two wonderful children, a great, challenging position with the State Dept. of Education, a beautiful home, and a loving and caring husband. I should be happy, but this whole thing with Roger just goes to show that at any time fate can pull the rug out from under you and leave you floundering. No, I'll not allow myself to be happy as long as there are people and forces that can pop my balloon and disappear like the wind. Such people and forces are, and always will be, a key part of reality. That's why I am not going around grinning and joking like some fool."

Dr. Sawyer shook his head and said, "Evvy, I prefer that you call me Dr. Sawyer as I feel it is very important in therapy for there to be a clear line between Doctor and patient."

Evvy responded, "Fine then call me Ms. Maynard, Dr. Sawyer."

"My goodness, you are combative, aren't you," was all Dr. Sawyer could say.

"I'm not combative, just as you want to keep things in perspective, so do I. Let's get started on this waste of time," was Evvy's response.

Dr, Sawyer said, "Very well, how is your sex life?"

Evvy said, "Fine." Roger intervened, "I know that you should be getting the information from Evvy, but "it" is not fine. It was great, as we probably averaged three and sometimes four times a week. Since this legal nightmare began several weeks ago, we attempted it twice and Evvy couldn't become even a little aroused. She hardly talks to our children any more. She use to ask them about school, help with Lola's homework, always attended the PTA meetings, and now she just doesn't take any interest in the children and their schooling. She would always ask me how my day went and I would ask her about her day, now there is only the most perfunctory conversation between us. Evvy was always reading, books, magazines and even the local paper, what there is of it, but now she finishes whatever she must do and retreats into the bedroom to lay across the bed and nap. This is why we are here, I feel like I've lost the light in my life, and I don't know what to do to rekindle it, not just for me but just as importantly our children."

Evvy, who sat silently staring at the corner of Dr. Sawyers desk, looked up and said, "Look I suppose I have been a little down lately, but there is good reason. Several weeks ago my ideal little world collided with reality, and I realized that nothing is permanent. Everything in our lives is transitory and can change in an instant. I just need time to adjust to this idea and in time I'll be good "old always smiling Evvy" again. I don't need this, It's a waste of Dr. Sawyer's time and our time and money. No disrespect Doctor, but I'm ready to go home." With that she was picking up her purse from along side of her chair.

Doctor Sawyer said, "I have listened to both of you and I believe you are wrong Evvy. You do have a serious problem which is what is frequently called "situational depression" it is a condition which is brought on by an event or occurrence which goes on and deepens as time passes. Contrary to your feelings Evvy, I don't feel this being "a little down" is going to go away with time, it will only become more pronounced until you will not be able to function as a Mother, Wife, or as a rising star in the State Department of Education. The larger problem is that I cannot help you if you are going to fight with every word I utter. I'll be very honest and tell you that this problem is connected with your husband's recent arrest, but I just feel that it is something deeper that perhaps you cannot even admit to yourself. I can help you with that, to get whatever it is out in the open so that we can deal with it."

Evvy looked at Roger and shook her head and said, "Roger, you know I have a Doctorate in Applied Psychology, and again, no harm intended, I feel that Doctor Sawyer is just resorting to the psychobabble that numerous years of medical training instills, and is imagining nonexistent problems. I have enough education and training to recognize that I do have some minor depression issues, but nothing that won't clear up in a couple of weeks at the most. Now if you're ready to drive me home, I'm ready to go."

Dr. Sawyer responded, "Look Evvy, I told you that I can't help you if you don't want to be helped. I don't think this is going to go away, even when the charges against Roger are dismissed which I understand from Roger is what is going to happen. Whatever the problem is, you have built a wall around yourself without any entrances, and it appears you are not allowing any trespassing. I wish you every success in dealing with this on your own, but until you want help, I can't help you."

Roger shrugged and said, "Well Doctor Sawyer, I'm sorry to have wasted your time. If you will send your bill to me, I will take care of it." Dr. Sawyer shook his head and said, "there is no bill as the session was totally unproductive. I'm sorry you came all the way down to Atlanta for nothing.

I hope things work out for both of you. If it appears at some point that I can help, please call me."

With that Roger rose and shook hands with Dr. Sawyer, and he and Evvy left the office for a silent ride home.

CHAPTER 21

The weeks passed quickly. Roger buried himself in his work as he was busy installing a data based operations program. It seemed there were problems at every turn, but it was starting to show results. At home, Evvy took a leave of absence from her employment and seemed to withdraw more and more into a shell. Without working or doing exercises any longer she was starting to put on weight. This further fed her depression, and her appearance started to reflect that Evvy didn't care.

As the trial date neared, Roger had several meetings with Rueben Jackman, who was increasingly optimistic. Two weeks before the trial Rueben asked Roger if he had briefed Evvy about the fact that she was to testify and that she should be prepared to show the court the small rose tattoo just above her left hip. Roger said he had not, but he would do so that evening. He explained to Rueben that his wife has been deeply depressed over the entire situation, and he was saving this information to hopefully cheer her up.

Roger arrived home about 6:30 that evening, and as had become the pattern whenever he worked late, there was a note on the counter in the kitchen that Evvy had fed the kids and Roger's dinner was in the microwave and she was laying down as she didn't feel well. Roger heard the TV on in the den and he found Lola and Davon watching a

Discovery channel special on elephants. He hugged them and asked if they had dinner, and they said yes. He chatted with them for a few more minutes and told them he was going to check on their Mom.

As Roger entered their bedroom, he saw Evvy laying across the bed in the dim light provided by a small ceramic boudoir lamp on the dresser. He noted that Evvy was still in her pajamas with her open house coat about her. Roger gently called Evvy and she stirred, rubbed her eyes and said, "Oh, you're home, did you eat?" Roger responded, "No not yet.

There is something that I need to tell you about." "More bad news?" Evvy sleepily asked.

"No this is very good news. You're going to have to testify at the trial and what you have to say and show is the clincher that will have the case thrown out of court. That is if you don't mind showing the court your rose tattoo on your left hip." Evvy sat up on the edge of the bed, "Whatever are you talking about?"

Roger said, "Do you remember the afternoon that you came down to look at the house and afterward, we went to my motel room and engaged in an afternoon of sex?" Evvy, now fully awake answered, that she did remember. Roger went on, "Well, someone had placed a hidden camera in the room and the DVD that was made from that recording is the DVD that the prosecutors say was Hanna and me. Whoever is behind this, edited the original so that it never shows the woman's face." Evvy gasped and Roger said, "You'll only be on the stand for ten minutes, and you'll only have to pull your waistband down an inch or two so that it can be verified." Evvy said, "Oh Roger, you mean you never had sex with that terrible woman? I must apologize to you, how could I have been so stupid as to not believe you. I was certain you had given into your desires and had been with her. What have I done?"

Roger asked, "What do you mean?" Evvy seemed at a loss for words for a moment, but then she replied, "I meant that I almost destroyed our marriage and threw away the years of trust we have in each other. I can't believe that I was so blind and stupid. How can I ever make it up to you?" Roger said, "Don't worry about it Evvy, nothing can ever change my love for you. I can't blame you for believing what everyone else believed." With that Evvy stood up and threw her arms around Roger shoulders and they kissed as Roger's arms encircled Evvy. They stood that way for several minutes as if neither of them wanted the moment to end. Finally Evvy said, "I didn't realize that she and I looked so much alike from the back."

Roger said, "Well I couldn't believe my eyes when I first started to watch it in Jackman's office. I couldn't figure out how they could have super imposed her body on mine as I knew above all else that I never was alone with Hanna in a motel room. Then I noticed your flowery blue blouse lying on the floor at the foot of the bed, and next I saw your white pleated skirt draped over the arm of the chair, and the time on the nightstand clock showing 2:30. It struck me like a thunderbolt, I was watching you and I having sex that wonderful afternoon we spent in the motel room. It is the little rose in the room that is going to make a lot of people look very stupid, and give us our lives back."

Evvy said, "Of course I'll testify, I don't mind showing my hip to the court, but it is going to be embarrassing to do after they show the video of me humping on top of you." "It isn't too bad as we'll stop it before your orgasm," Roger joked. They both laughed and Evvy said, "I'd love to do a repeat performance tonight after we get the kids to bed. I have longed to touch you and feel your lips on mine, to feel you inside of me." Roger said, "it's been a long time since they arrested me, I thought you had really lost it, I was so worried for you." Evvy said, "I just couldn't help myself, all I wanted to do is sleep and put this whole terrible thing out of my consciousness, I couldn't face what I,,, I mean what they said you had done. That you had slept with another woman. It was just unthinkable."

Roger said, "In a couple of weeks the trial will happen and I will be acquitted of all charges, at that point, we can all feel we're equal to everyone else and there will be no stigma over you, the kids, or me. Jackman feels that the civil suit against Greenville County, and the sheriff's office, should net us several hundred thousand dollars. If you wish, we can move away from here start over somewhere else, out of the south."

The Maynard family's life changed for the better that evening. Within a week Evvy had gone back to work and seemed to have that spark of life. She still seemed to have fleeting periods of melancholy, but she once again took an interest in Davie and Lola, helping them with their school projects and homework. She was again the passionate woman that Roger had married. Once more, life was good, at least until the prosecution's press release appeared in the local papers with a complete rehash of the case to that point. It made Roger sound like some sort of crazed killer. That is when the phone calls started again.

Evvy was always home by four thirty in the afternoon, about twenty minutes to a half hour after the school bus dropped Lola and Davon at the corner each afternoon. When Evvy opened the front door, she found Lola and Davon huddled under the dining room table, and Lola was sobbing. Evvy, knelt down and pulled the children into her arms and asked what was wrong. Davon spoke up and said, "A man said a lot of bad, mean things to Loly," a name Davon frequently called his big sister, and me. He said he was going to burn our house down and other bad stuff." Lola said, "Mommy we want to go home. This man came up to us at the bus stop and said, "Tell yo momma and daddy, if he is yo daddy, to pack up and go back north where all the other uppity niggers are who don't know their place. If you all don't we'll burn your goddamn fancy house down. Iff'n the judge don't string yo Daddy up, we will, yo'all tell em that." "Then he got in a car with some lady and they drove away. I'm scared Mommy."

Evvy comforted Lola and decided that she should call Roger and tell him what happened to the children, when the phone rang as she reached for it. She said hello and a voice on the phone said, "Is this the nigger ho of the house?", and Evvy slammed the phone down.

The phone rang again and the voice said "Don't yo hang up on me yo black bitch, I'll come over," and with that Evvy depressed the button on the cradle and laid the phone on the table with the dial tone sounding. She got out her cell phone and called Roger at the office. They discussed what had happened and Roger said he would call Jackman as Rueben said if there were any more threats, he would get protection for the family from the State Police. They agreed to go out to dinner and Roger said he would meet Evvy and the kids at Simple Simons House of Pizza.

The dinner was uneventful and the family enjoyed the brief respite. There were the usual stares and whispers whenever Roger was out in public. When the family was with him, it was even more pronounced. When they drove up to their home, there was a State Police car in front of the house, and as they pulled into the driveway, a Trooper got out of the car and approached their cars. Roger called to him "We're the Maynard family, we live here." The Trooper nodded, touch his fingers to his hat and returned to his car. Thus the first night of the siege began.

CHAPTER 22

It did turn out to be a siege. The rancorous, vulgar, threatening phone calls continued, and despite the State police efforts to trace the calls it was impossible as the calls were too short to trace. Roger found out that Jackman had connections with high officials in the State government and though them he obtained the protection at their home and the call tracing efforts. During the second week the State Police parked up the block and caught three men in a pick-up truck with a wooden cross, rags and gasoline to burn a cross on the lawn of the Maynard's home. Unfortunately, since they didn't wait for the men to actually place and set fire to the cross, there were no arrest, and the men walked away.

Another incident occurred a week later. The children had used the last of the milk in the morning so Evvy stopped on her way home from the office to pick up a gallon at the nearby WaWa store. As she waited at the checkout, a white woman, who was shabbily dressed came up to Evvy and said, "You the wife of that guy who stabbed the nigger whore to death?" Evvy was startled and all she could think to say was, "Leave us alone, he didn't do it." The woman scoffed and said, "You ain't no better than that nigger whore, move into the nigger section where you all belong." With that she turned and spit on Evvy's coat. Evvy started to cry and the

Vietnamese clerk said, "Don you cry. she bad lady." Evvy sniffled and wiped her tears and then the spittle running down her coat. She paid for her purchase and quickly left the store.

When she arrived home Evvy told the State Trooper on duty outside her home, and he asked a few questions and made notes on a note pad. As Evvy entered the house Lola ran up to her and threw her arms around her and sobbed, "Mommy, Mommy, some of the kids in my homeroom class said that Daddy is going to hang, and others said that he is going to die in the electric chair. Another boy said the Klan is going to get him. I'm so scared." Evvy hugged Lola and said, "Don't worry honey, we're going to be alright. and no one is going to hurt your Father. He did not do anything wrong and always remember the truth wins over lies every time. Now stop crying and forget all this nonsense your classmates are telling you as they are completely wrong. Wash your face and start on your homework." Lola reluctantly left her Mother's side and headed for the bathroom.

She called Roger and told him about the incidents. Roger said, "It must be a concerted effort to demoralize all of us. At lunchtime I went to my car to drive over to Smitty's Diner for lunch and the back tires of my car were flat as they had been slashed. I had asked Frank to go to lunch with me and we used his car. I called the State Police and they sent a trooper over who looked at the damaged tires, took photos and wrote a report on the incident. He said they would have slashed all four tires, but they only did the rear tires where they could not be seen since I had backed in and the rear of the car was against the wall. They have been replaced already as I called AAA and they took care of it. Thank God the trial is next week, then this harassment will end after the court dismisses all charges against me." They spoke of a couple other things and ended their phone conversation.

Two nights later, at about three in the morning they were awakened by an insistent knock on the front door, and the ringing of the chimes. Roger quickly got out of bed, slipped on his robe and answered the door. It was the Trooper who said, "I don't believe your home is in any danger, but someone has set fire to your shed in the rear. As soon as I saw the flames reflecting in your neighbor's windows, I ran to the back of your property but whoever did it was gone. I've called the fire department and they should be here any minute. I thought someone should be awake in the house just in case they try anything else. I recommend that you all stay inside." Roger said, "Alright we will stay inside." As Roger closed the door there was a loud crack and splintered wood from the top panel of the door showered down upon him. The Trooper who was halfway down the walk pulled his pistol and ran toward the hill in back of the homes on the opposite side of the street. Roger peeped from the side of a front window, shielded by the heavy drapes. He could see the Trooper with his flashlight scanning the hill top. Obviously who ever fired the shot was long gone and he rushed back to his car to call for backup.

The fire engines arrived a few minutes later and quickly extinguished the blaze which had eaten through the rear of the shed which faced the woods, and was quickly consuming the inside contents. In the morning the light revealed that it almost had reached a gas can and it had scorched the paint on the riding lawn mower. It could have been much worse, and it did get worse when Great Southern Homeowners Insurance Co. rejected all of the Maynard family's claims for reimbursement. Several days after Roger had sent in the bids for rebuilding the shed, and a few items destroyed in the fire, the replacement of the front door, and the two new tires, he received a letter from the insurance company. It was brief and to the point: "We are enclosing our check for $ 627.18, which represents the full refund of your recent premium. We are very sorry, but your application failed to provide your full names (your middle names were missing). If you read our Disclosure Statement which you signed, it plainly stated that all requested information must be provided as omissions of any information may cause this policy to become null and void. In addition we do not cover claims resulting from damages sustained in war or riots, as noted in the exclusion clauses. Thank you for your business. Signed James McNulty, Applications Examiner."

Roger was furious when he received the letter, He called Jackman and Ruben said, "Super, someone else to sue, and I will." The trial was due to start on Monday and it was a hectic week with several trips to Jackman's office in Atlanta for last minute preparations for the testimony to be given by Roger and Evvy.

On Thursday Roger was leaving the plant and was walking to his car when he heard someone call, "Mistah Roger, Mistah Roger, Can I talk to you for a minute?" As Roger turned around, he saw it was George Gaines, the plant janitor. Roger said, "Of course George, what can I do for you?

George replied, "Well Mistah Roger, all of us in the plant knows that yo is in trouble and I wanted to tell yo that I live two doors from the Williams home, and that family was always somthin else. When Jimmie and Hanna was growin up they was cop cars there every other day. Those kids were always in some kinda trouble, or there was some fight between their mother and whoever her man was at the time. I jes wanna say that I'se willin to to testify what kinda people they are, if yo think it would help you. I'se also want to tell yo thet all of the folks, blacks and whites, in the plant are prayin fo yo an your family, cause they feel yo are innocent."

Roger thanked George and told him he would let him know if he needed his testimony and to thank the employees in the plant for their support. As he drove home he realized that the plant had become a family, and that he would have to do everything he could to make the business a success and provide job security and good wages for all of the employees.

CHAPTER 23

The trial commenced at 9:00 o'clock sharp in the courtroom of the Honorable Judge James Clevenger. Everyone who could pack into the courtroom did so, as every seat was occupied, and the press presence represented just about every major city newspaper in the south. Judge Clevenger was known to be a strict judge who relied solely on precedent law. He was not apt to rule in any new directions, and he had never been overruled by the Appeals Court. He ran a tight courtroom and he took pride in that he had never presided over a mistrial.

The jury selection was a tedious process, and after all the questions and challenges by each side, they had twelve people for the jury and three alternative or back up jurors. During the brief recess after the jury was seated, Roger leaned over toward Jackman and asked how he felt about the final jury. Rueben smiled and said, "It's about as good as it gets once you get south of Maryland, half of them are probably Klan members and the other half are their relatives. Don't worry Roger, this case is never going to go to the jury."

The defense went first with their opening statement, and Rueben Jackman painted a picture of a model American family. A family that believed in success through hard work and education. A family, who due to their race and position, had been discriminated against and framed in a colossal conspiracy. He told the jury that the Prosecution will describe Roger as a philanderer and a vicious killer when Hanna Williams threatened to expose their alleged affair, and that they will claim that they have rock solid proof that there was an affair, but the prosecution is wrong. Jackman concluded his opening statement by admonishing the jury to look at Roger and Evona as a typical American family striving to provide a good home, and a fulfilling life for their children. His final words were, "Forget that they are black, or any different than any one of you."

The lead prosecutor, Glen Heller, delivered his opening statement, and true to Jackman's prediction, he described Roger as a man who, because of his education, position and wealth, felt above the law. He carried on an affair with a known part-time prostitute and when she confronted him with her video and a demand for money, Roger repeatedly and in cold blood, stabbed her to death in Hanna's own car, then threw her wounded body behind a dumpster in the rear of the motel where Hanna had a room. There hidden from the world, Hanna bled to death. The prosecution will show that Roger Maynard is a cunning heartless killer who thinks he is superior to all around him. He is without religion, as he and his wife do not attend any church and his children are being raised in a Godless home as they do not attend any Sunday school. Heller finished his opening statement to the jury with the words, "When we have presented all of the evidence to you, you will not have a shred of doubt that this man (he turned and pointed to Roger) should be put to death in the electric chair for this brutal and vicious murder."

After opening statements, Judge Clevenger ordered a two hour recess for lunch. When court resumed, the prosecution began presenting their case. Glen Heller first called George Scuggs to the stand. Scuggs was the manager of the motel. After all the formalities of establishing identity, employment, etc., Heller asked him to describe what happened the morning Hanna Williams body was discovered. Scuggs described how he approached the dumpster to empty the waste basket from the office, and he first saw a woman's shoe on the ground. Then he noticed marks in the soil, leading behind the dumpster like someone was dragging a body. Jackman objected as this was speculation. Judge Clevenger sustained the objection and Heller continued to ask Mr. Scuggs to describe exactly what he saw. George Scuggs seemed a little flustered, and stammered a bit describing the bloody body of Hanna Williams. Jackman did not cross examine.

Next came several detectives who testified to what steps they took to secure the area as a crime scene and how they searched in vain for any forensic evidence. Their testimony was professional and obviously well rehearsed and drew no objections from Jackman. The murder weapon had not been found. Deputy Detective Bruce Hazelit was the last to testify. He had conducted a search of the room which Hanna rented in the motel. The motel manager Mr. Scuggs had given his permission for the search, and "in fact" opened the door to the room for him. Hazelit described dusting the room for prints and going through Ms. Williams' belongings where he found two DVD, video discs. which were entered into evidence as Exhibits A1 & A2. The only other significant item was Ms. Williams' personal phone book, also entered into evidence as Exhibit B.

After the detectives, Heller called Dr. Evelyn McGraw, the coroner, to the stand. Again the prosecution went through the protocol of identification and a detailed description of her professional credentials. At that point it was late in the afternoon and Judge Clevenger recessed the court until 9:00 AM. the next morning. He admonished the Jurors not to discuss the case with anyone and to refrain from watching or reading any media coverage of the trial.

Chapter 24

Promptly at 9:00 the next morning, the Bailiff called the court to order and Judge Clevenger reminded the court that Dr. McGraw was still under oath. Thus began day two of Roger's trial.

Dr. McGraw was a very petite lady in her sixties, who had an extensive background as a general surgeon at the Charlotte Memorial Hospital in Charlotte, North Carolina. She had retired two years ago and accepted the position of County Coroner for Greenville as it was basically a part-time position. She was very thorough and precise in her testimony as she described the corpse of Hanna Williams. A black female, approximately five foot four, weighing one hundred and fifteen pounds, age thirty. Officially identified in the morgue by her brother, one Jamie Williams, and by dental records and her South Carolina State drivers license.

Heller next asked her if she could approximate the time of death. Dr. McGraw described the most accepted method which utilizes the temperature of the liver as a ratio to the ambient temperature where the body was discovered. As a result, Dr. McGraw estimated the time of death at about eight p.m. on the evening of December 1st. The next questions pertained to the cause of death. Dr. McGraw described the sixteen stab wounds, most of which were superficial. The one that caused Ms. Williams to bleed to death was a wound to the left side of the neck which severed the left carotid artery. It appeared to Dr. McGraw that this was not a premeditated murder, but rather one of rage as she had seen similar attacks in her years in general surgery at various hospitals.

Heller next asked if she could describe the weapon used in the attack. Dr. McGraw said, "the knife was definitely a serrated blade of about eight inches long, probably a kitchen knife. It is theorized that the attack took place in Ms. William's automobile while she was on the driver's side, that is behind the wheel. The direction of the wounds would be consistent with the attacker being in the passenger seat, to Ms. Williams right side." Heller said that was all he had to ask Dr. McGraw. It was now almost noon time. Judge Clevenger called for an hour and a half lunch break, and said when court resumed Mr. Jackman may cross examine if he wished.

After lunch Rueben approached Dr. McGraw on the stand and asked her, "Were there any marks such as birthmarks, tattoos, etc. on Ms. Williams?" Dr. McGraw took out a small notebook which she had referred to often during her prior testimony. She flipped through a few pages and said, "Yes, Ms. Williams had an irregular oval birthmark on the inside calf of her left leg about a inch and a half by two inches, there was a similar birthmark on her back, just below the left shoulder blade. There was also a tattoo of a rose about two inches in diameter on her right shoulder." Jackman pressed on "Are you certain there were no other tattoos anywhere else on her body?" Dr. McGraw somewhat agitatedly responded "Yes Mr. Jackman, I am certain there were no other tattoos." Rueben thanked Dr. McGraw and said he had nothing else at this time.

The balance of the afternoon was devoted to testimony from a night clerk from the hotel where Roger normally stayed before the family moved down. Heller asked Mr. Daryl Mathers, "If he had any recollection of Ms. Williams visiting Mr, Maynard's room during the times he stayed there?" Mr. Mathers said, "I recall one evening she came to the front desk and asked to see Mr., Roger. I called his room and he said no visitors, she could contact him at his office." "I see" Heller said and then he asked, "Do you know if Ms. Williams visited Mr. Maynard's room on other occasions?" Mathers said, "The motel is laid out like an *ell* and the office is on the opposite side from Mr. Roger's room, so I couldn't say for sure. Jackman objected and said, "I would like to ask that Mr. Mathers testimony of "so I couldn't say for sure" be stricken from the record as it implies there is a possibility." Judge Clevenger said "Overruled, let's be real, anything is a possibility Mr. Jackman. Heller smiled and thanked Mr. Mathers.

Judge Clevenger said "You may cross examine Mr. Jackman. Rueben looked over his yellow legal pad and asked, "Mr. Mathers did Mr. Maynard always have the same room?" "Why yes sir. he certainly did, he paid a monthly rate and said he wanted to do that as he could leave his clothes and stuff so he didn't have to carry so much luggage back and forth on weekends." "Now Mr. Mathers let me ask you this, did any tradesmen ever come to the motel in the evening when Mr. Maynard was not staying there?" "What do you mean? asked Daryl Mathers, Jackman said, "Well like someone to repair something in the room. maybe the air conditioner or such?" Daryl thought for a moment and said, "Why yes now that I think about it. Some guy came twice in the evening to fix the air conditioner in that room.

He said he had an emergency call on it and he was busy all day. and was just getting to it"

Heller was on his feet, objecting to the relevance of the line of questioning. Judge Clevenger said, "Mr. Jackman, I am also wondering where this is going as it seems totally disconnected from the charges against your client." Ruben replied, "I'm finished with this for now, I will tie it to some other testimony when the defense presents their case". "I hope you can, or I will have it stricken from the record," Judge Clevenger stated.

Next, Heller called Frank Bouchard. Frank had told Roger he was called to testify by the prosecution about the time Roger left the plant the evening of the murder. Roger thanked him and said just tell the truth. Frank was sworn in and took the stand. Heller asked him, "to tell the court what time Roger Maynard left the plant on that fateful evening." Frank replied, "That was the evening we were working on some new product designs for presentation to our marketing people the next day. We finished up fabricating the new mattresses at about six thirty, and Roger and I discussed them and a few possible changes until a few minutes after seven. I asked Roger if he wanted me to lock up and he said he had to do some more cost work on the new models, and that he would lock up. Shortly after, I had put my coat on and stuck my head in his office and asked if he needed any help. He said no and I left the plant."

"Now Mr. Bouchard, Did Mr, Maynard seemed distracted or worried?" Heller had no more than spoken the words when Jackman was on his feet objecting. "This calls for an opinion that Mr. Bouchard is not qualified to judge, he is not a psychologist." Judge Clevenger sustained the objection. Heller tried again, "Did Mr. Maynard seem to be his usual self?" Jackman started to stand and Judge

Clevenger said, "I'll allow it as he works with Mr. Maynard every day and he should know if he seemed normal" Jackman sat back down and Frank said "Yes, I did not sense anything different about him." Heller thanked Frank and Judge Clevenger bade Jackman to cross examine if he wished.

Jackman asked Frank how could he recollect the time so well, was there any possibility that it could have been earlier or later? Frank replied, Ï approve all time cards of the hourly employees, and I distinctly remember the four hourly employees who were working with us all punched out at six twenty-five, and I locked the plant side door behind them, and returned to the display room where we had set up the new models and had a discussion with Roger about potential production problems with one of the new models, and possible improvements to two of the other models. As I said, I went to my office, put on my coat and said goodnight to Roger. As I walked out and locked the door behind me I heard the Amtrak train heading southwest on its way to Atlanta. The track crosses a field about a quarter mile east of the plant. It is scheduled to leave Greenville at six forty-five and should pass our location about six fifty-five. I looked at my watch and it was seven oh six. It was running a few minutes late as usual." Jackman thanked Frank and said he had nothing further. Heller refused cross-examination.

Heller called Evona Maynard next. "Ms. Maynard, I called you as a witness for the prosecution, not to testify against your husband, but rather to just establish some times which might be in question. On the evening of December first, do you recall what time, Mr. Maynard arrived at your residence?" Evvy said, "I can't be sure but it I think it was a few minutes before nine o'clock." A murmur ran through the courtroom. Judge Clevenger glared out at the spectators and the murmur subsided as quickly as it arose. "How do you know that Ms. Maynard?" Heller persisted. "Well, I had forgotten some papers at my office that contained information I needed for a report that I had to present the next day. I got my kids settled down and in bed at eight thirty, and I drove over to my office which is about a ten minute drive from my home, picked up the papers and drove back to the house. I just about had time to fix a cup of tea when Roger came home." "Thank you, just one more thing, what was his appearance, did he act normal?"

Jackman was on his feet objecting to the line of questioning, "We should have refused the summons to testify, a wife does not have to testify against her husband. We permitted it only because there is nothing to hide and the prosecution said it was just to establish the time line, which Mrs. Maynard has done. Judge Clevenger said, "Your objection is sustained. Mr. Heller unless you have another question pertaining to a time issue, you're finished, and Mrs. Maynard may be cross examined, if Mr. Jackman wishes. Jackman replied, "Thank you, your Honor but we have no questions for this witness at this time.

Heller had a string of witnesses following Evona. There was the receptionist from Roger's office to testify that Ms. Williams had visited him at the plant. Jackman cross examined to ask if the door to his office remained open during the woman's very short visit. Then Heller had a waitress testify that some months earlier she had seen Roger and Ms. Williams together in a local restaurant. On cross, Jackman asked her if Mr. Maynard had acted romantically with Ms. Williams. The waitress said, "No, it was more like he was interviewing her." Jackman had several other questions to which he knew the answers would further dispel any notion that this was a romantic tryst. After this he concluded his cross examination.

Shortly thereafter, Heller announced that he had a video to show the jury that would speak louder than all of the witnesses. It shows that there was a great deal more going on between Roger Maynard and Ms. Williams than just being acquaintances. Heller said that would conclude the prosecution's case. Jackman asked, "Your Honor, would it be possible to recess for today and start fresh in the morning?" Judge Clevenger said, "It is late. and I believe the jury has heard enough for one day. Court will resume at 9:00 am. So ended day two of the trial.

CHAPTER 25

As court resumed at nine the following morning, a staff from the prosecutor's office was busy setting up a screen and a digital projector. They had just finished when Judge Clevenger took the bench. Heller said, "if it pleases the court, we will now show you a very graphic video of Hannah Williams and Roger Maynard engaged in a sexual act. This is the case containing the DVD marked Exhibit A1 which Deputy Detective Hazelit testified he removed from Ms. Williams room the day after the murder. I will now insert the DVD in the player and in a moment we will, without a doubt, prove what the defense has denied, a most definite and intimate relationship between Ms. Williams and Mr. Maynard.

Jackman rose to his feet and said, "If I may address the court, I will save the court's time by stipulating that the defense has previously viewed the DVD in discovery, and it does show Mr. Maynard engaged in a sexual act. Judge Clevenger said that the stipulation is granted. Heller was somewhat disturbed as this was the prosecution's last piece of evidence they were presenting and he had hoped it would leave a lasting impression on the jury. He started to say, "Your Honor we..." Judge Clevenger asked, "Is there a problem Mr. Heller?" Heller said no and sat back down. Judge Clevenger then asked if the prosecution had any further evidence or testimony to offer. Heller stood and said "No Your Honor, the State rests it's case."

Jackman stood and said, "I have one witness to call, Mrs. Evona Maynard. The Bailiff called Mrs. Maynard. Evvy entered the courtroom and was sworn in again. As she took the stand, Jackman strode to a position at the rail of the jury box, He asked, "Mrs. Maynard, can you tell the court a little about yourself and your family. Evvy, proceeded to tell of her background, having grown up in a large family in Newark, New Jersey. Attended Rutgers and earned her Bachelor of science degree at twenty-two and her Doctorate in Applied Psychology at twenty-five. She met Roger the following year and after a six month courtship they were married. Two years later her first child was born, Lola, and 6 years later Davon was born. She quickly summarized her employment history, and then Jackman asked her, "If she had a document in her possession that would have a bearing on this case?" She answered in the affirmative. He asked could she give it to the clerk to enter into evidence after Mr. Heller has an opportunity to view it. The Clerk approached the stand and Evvy handed her a slip of paper which appeared to be a receipt of some sort. The clerk took it to Heller who examined it very closely.

Jackman asked Evvy if she would tell the court what it is. Evvy said, "When I was twenty-three, one of my best friends was being married and we, that is ten other friends and I, held a bachelorette party for her. During the course of that evening we happened upon a tattoo parlor and we decided that we would all get a tattoo of a rose and call ourselves the Dozen Roses. The next day I had strong misgivings about having a tattoo and I held on to the receipt with the idea of seeing if the parlor could remove it. I called and they said it was a painful, prolonged, and expensive process to remove it, so I forgot about it. I have no idea why, but I saved the receipt."

Heller was on his feet waving the slip of paper and making an objection for the relevancy of the testimony and to entering the receipt as evidence. Jackman said, "I will show the relevancy in a few minutes." Judge Clevenger bade the two attorneys to the bench and asked Jackman, "Where is this going? I hope you have an answer as I am about to sustain Mr. Heller's objection to both the testimony and the request for making this piece of paper a piece of evidence." Heller started to say, "this is the second time that....," but Judge Clevenger cut him off and said, "the court is handling it Mr. Heller. Jackman calmly, "Said if Mr. Heller would be so kind as to have his people darken the court and show his DVD, we will demonstrate the relevance."

The courtroom was darkened with only the indirect ceiling lights remaining lit. The Jury was on the edge of the seats to get the best view possible. Heller was fidgeting at the table as his people prepared the Digital projection device. He felt a knot in his stomach. He had a sinking feeling that there was something on the DVD that was going to kill his case, but he could not think of what it could be, Finally, the technician at the projector signaled that it was ready. Heller said, "Mr. Jackman will tell you what to do, it's his show."

Jackman ask the technician to start the DVD and stop after thirty seconds. The grainy images on the screen sharpened and by the time the DVD was paused, it displayed a black man and woman kissing although the woman's face was hidden by Roger's head and shoulders. Jackman asked to skip a minute into the DVD and when the images reappeared, they were disrobing with clothing being tossed helter-skelter. In no instance could one see the woman's face. The next images filled the screen displaying Roger with the woman astride him engaged in intercourse. Jackman asked that the video be paused and if the technician could zoom in on an area of the screen. He said he could and Jackman ask him to zoom in on the left hip of the woman. As he did a mark became obvious and as the image grew larger one could see that it was a tattoo of a rose about two inches in diameter. Again a murmur swept through the courtroom. Jackman said, "You may turn off the projector, and turn on the lights. Thank you."

Jackman approached the witness and ask her to stand and pull down the waistband of her white skirt. He asked Mr. Heller to verify the existence of the rose tattoo on Mrs. Maynard's left hip. Mr. Heller said "The prosecution will stipulate to the existence of the tattoo on Mrs. Maynard's left hip." Jackman then asked Mrs. Maynard to sit and he asked her, "Could you tell the Jury if there is any significance to the blue flowered blouse and the white pleated skirt you are wearing?" Evvy answered "Yes they are the same clothes that I wore the afternoon you observed on the video. Jackman said he had nothing further for the witness, and Judge Clevenger ask Heller if he wished to cross examine. He declined.

Jackman announced that he did have one more witness to call, a Mr. Robert Fallston.

The Bailiff called the gentleman from the witness ready area and a tall, well dressed man entered the courtroom. After he was sworn in Jackman ask him to tell the court of his occupation and credentials. He testified that he was the owner and operator of Fallston Investigative Services, LLC. He spent three years as an electronics technician for the LA police department, and five years with the Atlanta Criminal Investigation Division in a similar position, prior to starting his own business. Jackman said, "I provided you with the

DVD marked Exhibit A2, courtesy of the prosecution and asked you to examine it and offer your comments on it. Could you tell the court what you found?" Fallston spoke with confidence as he related, "The DVD is not a direct camera to DVD copy. The record and delete commands leaves an electronic marker in the disc. This DVD was very heavily edited, obviously to avoid showing the woman's face." Jackman was pacing and again paused in front of the jury box, and asked, "Can you tell the court anything about the camera and how this invasive video was recorded?"

"Of course." answered Fallston. "It was recorded with a Gotcha Corp camera or a similar make. From the angle of the view, it was obviously hidden in a ceiling heat and AC vent and was probably activated automatically with a capacitance sensor switch which was set to turn the camera on when more than one person enters the room. This a very common method of secretly operating a camera or other recording device." "Thank you Mr. Fallston. Your witness Mr. Heller", Jackman said as he returned to the defense table. Heller remained seated and asked, "Mr. Fallston you have used terms such as "probably, and obviously", the court operates on truth and facts, not guesses. How sure are you of your testimony here today?" Fallston said, "I'm certain to the extent that the camera was in a fixed position, that a great deal of editing was done on the video, and that the set-up was inexpensive and very simple. It was not a sophisticated system. I feel confident that my testimony is as accurate as can be made with just a DVD copy as evidence." Heller thanked him and said he had nothing further.

Jackman said, "if it would please the court, I would like to tie some loose ends together as I said I would. If you will recall Mr. Mathers the motel night clerk testified that a person visited the motel room of Mr. Maynard on two occasions, in the evening when Mr. Maynard was not in town, to repair the air conditioner. We believe that this person planted the camera and the switch to activate it. A second visit was obviously made to remove the camera and the recording. You heard Dr. McGraw testify that Ms. Williams had only one tattoo on her body, coincidentally, a rose on her right shoulder. None on her hip as Mrs. Maynard displayed both in the video and in this court. The defense entered a receipt into evidence showing the tattoo on Mrs. Maynard's hip is years old. The defense contends that this was a complete set-up by someone to discredit Mr. Maynard. Unfortunately, something went terribly wrong and Ms. Williams paid with her life, but my client had nothing to do with that. As a result of the preponderance of evidence, we make a motion for the dismissal of all charges against Roger Maynard."

Judge Clevenger called a recess and asked the attorneys to come to his office. As they entered his office, Judge Clevenger stopped at the corner of his desk and said, "This is the most botched prosecution I have ever witnessed in my court room. Mr. Heller, you apparently relied completely on the sheriff's office and evidence without doing any investigating yourself. I am dismissing the jury and all charges against Mr. Maynard. The incompetence of your office and the sheriff's department is without precedent. I feel that you could not convict Jack the Ripper if you had a jury who witnessed him in action. You and the sheriff's department will be lucky if Mr. Jackman doesn't sue your eyeballs out." Jackman and Heller remained silent and allowed Judge Clevenger to finish venting his rage. They then returned to the courtroom.

Judge Clevenger spoke to the court, "Members of the jury, the public, and the press, in view of the evidence presented by the defense in this court room today, I am dismissing all charges filed against Mr. Roger Maynard, with the apologies of the court as with a molecule of prudence and common sense on the part of the prosecution, this rush to judgment would never have occurred. An obviously good man and his family have been seriously maligned and degraded by groundless accusations. I am therefore dismissing the jury and thank them for their efforts and time. Court is adjourned."

CHAPTER 26

More than two dozen reporters swarmed around Jackman and Roger, Jackman had a prepared press release which reiterated the comments that he made in court. He did have a final paragraph which was not spoken in court it read, "We do not have a crystal ball to offer to the sheriff's office, but we uncovered evidence that Mr. Jamie Williams, the younger brother of the deceased Hanna Williams was overheard having a confrontation with his sister in the days just before her murder. In addition we would recommend that the Sherriff may want to look at the individual against whom the Sperling Mattress Company has a very large law suit pending. There are motives here that bear investigation instead of the knee jerk response that the black man did it."

Frank heard the news on the radio and told the employees that, "If they like fried chicken or pizza, don't bring lunch the next day as the company was buying lunch to celebrate Roger's exoneration." A cheer arose in the plant that was heard above the noise of the machinery. The local radio station asked Jackman and Roger to come on the "It's Happening Now", a daily talk show. Jackman gave them a taped statement as he had to be in court the day of the show. Roger and Evvy went on and in addition to answering questions, they thanked their friends, neighbors, and the employees at the plant, for standing by them through this troubled time.

That evening the phone rang and Roger answered it. A voice said "I'm the local Klan leader. and I just want to tell you, you'll have no further problems with us. You and your family were done a real injustice. We're sorry if we disrupted your lives." With that the call disconnected and the caller was gone. Some of the neighbors brought food to Roger and Evvy as they thought that with all the commotion with reporters that they would not have time to prepare a meal Sherriff Hardy stopped by to apologize and get some further information on the several leads that were mentioned in Jackman's press release. Roger and Evvy were cordial and they even offered Hardy a cup of tea or coffee, which he declined. The State trooper who had been guarding their home most nights also dropped in to make sure everything was alright. It appeared life was going to get back to normal, and the nightmare was finally over.

The weeks passed quickly and Roger was deeply engrossed in his work at the plants. His level of acceptance among his managers and the plant employees was excellent, After much haggling Newfeld had approved a million and a quarter equipment and renovation budget for the Southern division. Roger's sales staff were opening an average of forty new accounts per month, and the business was booming. His salesperson in Florida was the most prolific with almost thirty new accounts each month. Freight costs to Florida were actually hindering even greater sales growth, and Roger started thinking of trying to acquire a plant in the Sunshine state. A supplier to Sperling told Roger that, "Although it isn't on the market, there is an independent bedding plant for sale in Jacksonville called Sun State Mattress Co." This was what Roger was looking for, and after a phone call to the owner, a Mike Bucanti, Roger was making arrangements to fly into Jacksonville.

CHAPTER 27

Roger had a mid morning flight and told Evvy he would be gone for at least two days as he wanted to evaluate the equipment and inventory. He left on Tuesday morning and returned on Thursday evening and as he entered the house, he could tell something was not right. Breakfast dishes were in the sink and on the countertop, the beds were unmade, and no one was home. Evvy's car was not in the garage and Roger finally spotted a hastily scribbled note laying on Evvy's computer keyboard. It read, "Roger, Something terrible has happened and I have taken Lola and Davie back to Newark to stay with my Sister. I'll explain more when I get back tomorrow. Love, Evvy."

Roger called Evvy's cell phone and she answered on the fourth ring, Roger asked, "What has happened, are you and the kids alright?" Evvy answered that, "I am at my sister's and the children are fine, but I can't talk about it now. I'll see you tomorrow, when I get home. I love you and don't worry." With that she disconnected and Roger was left with a dead cell phone in his hand. "Don't worry! Don't Worry!" Roger thought what else can I do. This was so unlike Evvy. Usually she discussed any drastic actions with me, and this was drastic in Roger's mind.

He cleaned up the house, made the beds and was straightening up when he picked up today's edition of the

Greenville Sentinel. The headline was "Jamie Williams Charged With Murder of his Sister" The article went on to say that he had been taken into custody yesterday and charged with the murder of his sister, Ms. Hanna Williams. The sheriff's office reported, "That they learned he had a violent quarrel with his sister several days prior to her body being found on December 2nd, and that his prints were found on her car. Public Defender Junior Stebbins was assigned to defend Williams, but said he would not be able to comment at this time." Roger thought to himself, "It looks like Sheriff Hardy finally got around checking the lead I gave him."

The next day dragged by with each hour seeming to be a day. Roger had a morning phone call from Evvy to tell him that she would be home around six in the evening. Again she would not discuss the problem, only not to worry and she loved him. Roger found it hard to concentrate, but none the less he wrote a lengthy report to Isaac Newfeld, providing a complete picture of the business opportunity that Sperling would have in purchasing the Jacksonville plant, along with his recommendations for a fair purchase price. Even with all of this, his mind constantly kept going back to Evvy and what could be the problem.

CHAPTER 28

Roger left early so that he would be home when Evvy arrived. He was having a cup of coffee when Evvy walked in. They fell into an embrace and Evvy said, "Let me get my coat off and make a cup of coffee as I need it badly." Roger sat in his recliner and Evvy sat across from him balancing her coffee. Roger started to ask "What is..." and Evvy cut him off and said, "It's complicated. I should have told you this months ago when it happened. Did you see where they have arrested Jamie Williams for his sister's murder?" Roger said, "Yes I saw the paper, but what does all this have to do with you taking the kids out of school and up to your sister, I don't understand."

Evvy pushed off her shoes and said, "What it has to do is that I am going to confess to that bitches murder, I can't let an innocent man have his life ruined by something he didn't do. I don't want the children here at this time, particularly Lola. I've messed up all of our lives." With this Evvy could hold the tears back no longer. She started sobbing and Roger went to her side and caressed her while he asked whatever was she talking about. Evvy took a tissue from the box on the table and wiped her tears. She was still sobbing but through the sobs she related the events of the evening of December first.

"I was a few minutes later than usual getting home that afternoon. The children were already home and before I could get my coat off the telephone rang. Lola answered it and brought the phone to me as I was hanging my coat in the closet. She said some lady wanted to speak with me. I took the phone and said hello, and woman's voice said "are you Mrs. Maynard?" I said, "Yes, who is this. She responded, "I'm your friend, baby. and I am going keep you from being very embarrassed. I want you to meet me at the Twilight Motel, its right off the first service road on I85 after you cross the Columbia Pike, and Sugah, bring some cash with you, like five hundred. Five Ben Franklins will be fine. When you pull into the motel parking lot stay to your right and drive in back of the motel. Be here at six o'clock, park in back of the Honda Civic near the dumpster. Don't miss out on this baby as this will be on sale at a higher price after tonight. So tell me you'll be here, I'll look for you." I asked, "what are you talking about?" She said, "If you all love your man and your family you just get your ass out here at six. You'll find out all about it then."

"I said I would meet her and hung up. I quickly made dinner for Davie and Lola and told them I had to go out for a little while but I wanted them to be good and go to bed at seven-thirty if I was not back by then. I left the house a little early and stopped at the bank and drew out five hundred dollars through the ATM. It was a few minutes before six, and almost dark, when I arrived at the motel. I pulled into the back and a saw an older silver Honda Civic. As I stopped in back of it, a black woman got out of the car. She walked up to my car and I rolled down the window." She said, "I figured yo is a smart woman and wouldn't want to miss this sale." I asked what was she talking about. She said, "Sugah you-all get out and come over to my car, I've got a little movie to show you."

"I left my car and got in the passenger side of her car. It smelled of stale fast food and cigarette smoke. Wrappers, cups, and bags littered the back seat and floor of the car. She had one of those portable DVD players propped up in the middle of the front seat As she fiddled with the controls she said, "Baby this is the first five hundred dollar movie you-all ever gonna see." I reached into my purse to make sure the money was still there, and I felt the handle of the knife I had put in my purse before leaving the house, it was the one that has been missing and you ask me about every once in a while. I brought it for protection in case this was some sort of a scam to rob me.

The picture started coming up on the small screen, and it looked like a poorly photographed love scene I couldn't see her face, but I did see your face. I gasped when I saw the shot of you laying naked on the bed with an erection. As I watched, the woman who was also nude crawled on the bed and mounted you. She let it run for another few seconds and said "Honey, I think you-all have seen five hundred dollars worth." With that she hit some buttons and the screen went blank and the DVD drawer popped open and she took the DVD and said "Yo give me the five hundred and this little baby is yours. Yo know, yo is a lucky woman, that man sho know how to please a woman, and she laughed. At that point I just lost it. I didn't even know what I was doing, I had the knife in my hand and I was stabbing at her. She had her hands at her side trying to protect herself and I saw her hand get cut. She dropped the DVD and called me a crazy whore and to stop it. The DVD player fell on the floor and I made a lunge across the seat and the knife stuck in the side of her thigh. Everything is a blur as I grabbed the DVD and the DVD player. Hannah was crying and said look what you've done. I remember scrambling out of the car. I remembered that there was woods all in back of the dumpster and I threw the DVD player as far as I could. I don't remember much until somehow I became aware that I was sitting in our driveway and the motor was running.

I turned off the car and tried to compose myself. It was only six forty-five and the kids were still up. I gave them a snack and helped them get ready for bed. Lola wanted to know why they had to go to bed so early and I told her I didn't feel well and I needed to relax awhile as I had to do some work for the office. They're great kids and they did as they were told. Later still in a daze, I examined my purse and found the DVD which I broke into countless pieces and buried in the trash. Then you came home. I wanted to beat on you and ask how could you do it. How could you betray everything that we have between us. But, I remained the dutiful wife and you never suspected. The next day you were arrested for the woman's murder. I almost confessed then and there, and when I found out it was a video of you and I making love, I was devastated and elated all at once. I realized the senseless thing I had done all for nothing. I felt as though I had destroyed our lives. This is really what made me so depressed for awhile."

Roger crossed the room and hugged Evvy and said, "You may have cut Hanna's hand and you remember stabbing her in the thigh, but neither of those wounds would be considered fatal. The woman was stabbed sixteen times, do you remember doing that? Evvy sobbed and said, "I don't remember, but I must have. I want you to take me to the sheriff's office tomorrow and I'll turn myself in." Roger said, "Whoa!, you'll do no such thing. The first thing we'll do is talk to Rueben Jackman. In addition I think you should have a serious session with Dr. Sawyer." Evvy didn't feel any of this would change the fact that she had taken a life, but she agreed to follow Roger's advice. It was a long emotionally draining evening and they turned in early.

CHAPTER 29

It took three days before they could catch up with Jackman. Fortunately, that was because he was able to change his flight plans and fly into the Greenville/ Spartanburg airport. He was able to give Evvy and Roger two hours and twenty minutes as that was the length of his layover before a commuter flight boarded for Atlanta. Roger let Evvy tell her story and as Rueben listened he asked an occasional question and was making notes on his ubiquitous yellow legal pad. When she finished she added, "And that's why I want turn to myself in." Roger said, "We have an appointment with Dr. Sawyer tomorrow evening. I think Evvy should talk to him as she doesn't remember anything after stabbing Hanna Williams in the leg and grabbing the DVD, and the DVD player. That doesn't account for fifteen other stab wounds." Jackman said, "Sawyer is a good man, one of the best psychiatrists in Atlanta, and I think it's a great idea. I was going to suggest a psychiatric examination as the question of Evvy's consciousness between her being in Hanna's car and finding herself in your driveway was foremost in my thinking. Have your appointment with Sawyer and have him send a complete report to my office as soon as possible, and I will be in touch with you."

As Jackman was packing up his briefcase, a short, casually dressed man, walked up to him and said, "Rueben,

I thought that was you." They exchanged some pleasantries and stepped aside. Rueben returned to Evvy and Roger, and said, "He's an old friend of mine, and he offered me a ride back to Atlanta in his jet, so I have to leave you now." They said their goodbyes and then they were alone. Roger said he felt much better having had the meeting with Jackman, but Evvy was still very sullen as she repeated several times, "I took a life, I took a life. Nothing can change that."

The following morning Roger left early for the office as he planned to leave at noontime to pick up Evvy and start the trip to Atlanta. He was behind his desk sorting through reports when his cell phone rang. It was Newfeld and he was very enthused about purchasing the Jacksonville plant that Roger had recommended. He said, "Roger, I'd like you to fly down there this afternoon and start negotiations." Roger told him he couldn't as he had very pressing personal business, but that he would call and set up an appointment with Mike Bucanti, the owner of the Sun State Mattress Company. Newfeld was disappointed but he said fine. Roger called, but the earliest that Bucanti was going to be available was early the next week.

The drive to Atlanta was tense. They stopped at a Waffle House near Sawyer's office for a quick dinner. Evvy hardly touched her food, and her mood was very low. Roger asked if she was going to cooperate with Dr. Sawyer this time, and she answered, "Yes, of course, I am not trying to hide a secret this time." The meeting with Sawyer was much more cordial and relaxed. He asked Roger to wait in the waiting area as he was going to put Evvy under hypnosis.

After the session, Evvy was jubilant as she told Roger that she remembered everything now. She remembered that she started to pull the knife out of Hanna's thigh, but

Hanna pushed her hand away and said, "Leave it bitch, you're going to pay for this!"

Evvy continued, "I was sick to my stomach and I felt like I might pass out, so I climbed out of the car and I found the DVD player was still in my hand and I flung it as far as I could into the woods. I started my car and started driving for home, I made a wrong turn into our neighborhood and I turned around in driveway at the third house from the corner, and a man came out on the porch. I called out, "sorry I made a wrong turn." I recall everything now in detail, I did not kill that woman. She was very much alive when I left her." Evvy returned to her position at the Board of Education office the following day. The same day she called her sister and told her to put the children on a plane the next day as everything was fine now. Lola and Davie arrived back without incident and the family was complete again.

For the first time in almost a week, Roger was able to work with his full energy and concentration. He worked out various models of different purchase prices for the Jacksonville plant and ran analysis's of the return on investment in each scenario. This was work which he enjoyed, and the week passed quickly.

Several days later, Jackman called and told Roger to tell Evvy, "Do not, Do not turn herself in, or talk to anyone other than Roger about what happened." He continued, "That based on the report that Doctor Sawyer sent, I could get Evvy off without even trying. Besides that I have heard that Jamie Williams has failed two lie detector tests, and that the States Attorney's office was preparing an indictment for murder in the first degree. It appears that they are satisfied that he is the murderer of his sister. I also heard that they found what they believe to be the murder weapon in Jamie's apartment. Just tell Evvy to keep quiet and forget about the incident, Perhaps she gave the woman what she deserved, no more, no less. In any event, she has nothing to confess. I expect to have a court date shortly for our civil suit against the sheriff and City of Greenville. We want to see that they get what they deserve." Roger felt very good about the conversation and he could hardly wait to tell Evvy.

Roger had no sooner hung up from Jackman's call when he had a call from Thomas Hennings of Bryce, Hennings and Smith, Sperling's attorneys. Thomas told Roger that a trial date was now set in the 4th circuit court in Columbia, South Carolina on the following week. He pointed out that he had a great deal of testimony to go over with Roger, and ask if he could come to their office in Charlotte the next day. Roger agreed and spent the next five days with Thomas Hennings and his partner Douglas Bryce. He commuted daily and the 105 mile each way was a real chore as he did not arrive home until well after seven each evening. He was very satisfied since he felt that they had an solid case against Dave Atkins and Elwood Austin.

CHAPTER 30

The trial against Atkins and Austin opened the following Monday morning in the 4th Circuit Federal Court in Columbia. It was to be a bench trial, presided over by Federal Judge Thomas Kilpatrick. Sperling Mattress Inc. was the plaintiff and Dave Atkins and Great International Foam, Inc., and Ellwood Austin were the defendants. The defendant's attorneys were George Mason and Wallace Scuggs. Thomas Hennings made the opening statement claiming overpayments of $ 34,878.00 and $ 250,000.00 to cover returns of defective mattresses due to sub grade foam supplied by the defendant. In addition Sperling was asking for five million dollars for defamation of its name due to poor quality mattresses, and all attorney fees and court costs.

The testimony was long and tedious citing hundreds of invoices, Surveys of local foam prices offered by eight other manufacturers serving the area of the four plants over the period of time. The logging of exhibits and supporting testimony filled the first two days of the trial, The audit of the previous five years of the books of Southern Bedding, Inc. by Jamison and Clark accountants took another day resulting in irrefutable evidence that Ellwood Austin's old company kept two sets of books which resulted in massive tax savings for Austin and millions in undeclared income.

It also aided Austin in painting a rosy financial picture for Sperling's purchase of the company.

A similar audit of Great International Foam's books displayed gross collusion in kickback schemes with several customers as well as Southern Bedding. It showed a method of invoicing high to its customers, and for its accounting purposes invoicing low or at average prices for the books, and actually billing the customers much higher prices. The differences were skimmed off by Dave Atkins to pay huge kickbacks to those customers who participated, as well as line his own pockets with the tax free income.

The tests of the foam quality by recognized testing laboratories showed further deceptive practices by decreasing the density of the foam, but selling it as a more premium product.. Much of the foam which Atkins sold to Southern and later to Sperling was ten to thirty percent under the density that it was labeled. Roger testified as to the deleterious effects of using under specification foam, with the customer dissatisfaction with their mattresses, and ultimate returns due to the less dense foam taking an early compression set, creating large, and uncomfortable depressions in the mattress surfaces.

Ray Crocker testified as he promised and effectively described the kickbacks at Southern Bedding. Dave Atkins and Ellwood Austin were both called to testify, and each of them took the fifth amendment which grants one the right to refuse to testify if there is a possibility that it may tend to incriminate one. Frank testified to the return of defective mattresses and the cost of such returns to Sperling. By the time the trial was over, Judge Kilpatrick awarded Sperling the full amount of their claims, plus he added one million dollars in punitive damages.

For Roger the best thing to come out of the trial was Hanna's phone book which somehow was resurrected from the evidence files of Roger's trial for murder. It never came out at his trial because everyone accepted it for what it seemed to be, a telephone book. As Roger examined it he found the back half of the book was a calendar and Hanna made copious notes about her daily activities. An entry on the date that she forced herself on Roger at his dinner, read, "Mr A gave me two hundred to screw Roger Maynard, and promises me another three hundred if he gets some good pictures. Met Mr. Maynard and tried my best to get him into bed, but he wouldn't buy into it at all. He seems to be a real straight arrow"

Another entry relates her failure to even entice him to have dinner with her as Mr. A really wants to smear Roger and maybe get him fired. This time she was offered "five hundred big ones again" by Dave. This phone book would clear any remaining doubt that anyone held that Roger was involved with Hanna or her murder. Roger called Jackman after the trial and told him of the book and its contents. Jackman was ecstatic. He said, "this would be the ticket to a huge personal law suit against Dave Atkins for attempts to defame Roger's character and ruin him." He told Roger he would subpoena the document at once. This would be another forthcoming court episode for Dave Atkins and was sure to cost him many more dollars.

CHAPTER 31

Meanwhile in the labyrinth of halls and rooms in the basement of the Greenville Municipal Building, A small group of people sat around a conference table. Jamie Williams was in leg manacles and hand cuffs, and an armed guard stood behind him. Others present were Public Defender, Junior Stebbins, Sheriff Hardy, Deputy Detective Hazelit, and representing the DA's office was Heller. Sheriff Hardy read the preamble to a confession into a tape recorder, giving the date, time, names of those present, and the case number. He then addressed the prisoner, "Alright Jamie, we want you to start at the beginning and give us a complete picture of what happened on the night of December 1st., last year, just as you told me earlier."

Jamie said, "Furs of all, I want somethang on this here recordin that says cause I'm pleadin guilty, yo all callin it manslaughta and I wonn fry in de chair." Junior Stebbins spoke up and said, "That will not be necessary Jamie, as I have already signed off on a plea bargain agreement that changes the charge to manslaughter. Jamie said, "Ok yo say so man.

Jamie started his confession, "Well, bout six thirty that night, I gits a call on my cell, an it mah sistah, Hanna. She say Jamie yo need to come help me, ah needs help, ah been stabbed. Ah says aam not talkin to yo. Yo see we had had a big fight, couple days befo, cuz she had money an wooden loan me a damn Jackson. I'd of paid her back cuz I had a job I was goin to start the followin week. Anyway she tell me foget the fight, she need me to take her to a Doc that dozen report stab woouns. I tells her ahm about to get it on with a sweet youn thang, an it was de trut. We bote were naked an reddy to go. Hanna say I don care what yo doin, git yo black ass ova here. I gotta knife, stickin in me an ahm in my car behine the motel. I tell this lady ahm wif that ah be back soon an wait fo me. I gits mah fren, big Ed Gordo to drive me ova, an he drops me off, an says he be back ina hour. I sees mah sistah's cah an I opens de door an she say, look wat some bitch did to me. I looks an she got a knife stickin outa her leg. I ass why don yo pull it out, she say it hurt too bad. I tells her I know a Doc that take care of it, but ah needs two big Ben Franklins. She say all she got right now is fifteen dollahs. I tells her fogeta bout it.

She starts goin nutso, man. Callin me names, cussin me. She starts swingin her pokeebook and somethang init was hard. It hit me ina eye an I thought ah was blinded. Ah was high as ah had smoked some meth an a couple weeds earlier. Ah jus loss it. Ah pulled that knife outa her leg an ah started stabbin her lak ah was crazy. Finely she got still an I sees her neck bleedin bad, man an ah scared. Sos ah pull her outa de cah and she look lak dead. Ah pulls her body in back of the dumpster thang and ah take her cah an take off. I finds Big Ed an he follow me while ah drap off her cah. Ah wipe all mah prints off an Big Ed don know what goin down, but he is a good fren. Thass about it. Till yo all ass me to dentify her at de morgue. Ah was jes goin on wif my life when one day yo all arress me.

Ahm sorry I kilt mah sistah, but man she could be a real bitch. Always tellin me ahm no good an shit lak that.

Ah diden mean to do it, man but she made me lose it that night." Heller says, "I have a question Jamie, did she say who stabbed her before you arrived?" Jamie responded, "No suh, all she say is some bitch stabbed her. She always had somethang goin on wif other people. She was not a nice lady."

Sheriff Hardy asks if anyone else has any questions. Everyone at the table shakes their head or mumbles no. Sheriff Hardy tells the guard to take Jamie back to his cell. Heller is packing up his portfolio, as he tells Junior Stebbins that his office will notify him as soon as the full plea bargain agreement is typed up with Jamie's statement, and a hearing date is set.

CHAPTER 32

Several weeks later the headline of the Greenville Sentinel proclaimed "Brother Pleads Guilty To Murder of His Sister." The accompanying story provided full details of Jamie's confession. The court sentenced him to a fifteen to twenty year term, to be incarcerated at Stillman State Prison in Columbia, South Carolina. This was the news that Evvy and Roger had been waiting for. To celebrate, they took the children with them to the best steak house in Charlotte. While they were en route to Charlotte, Jackman called on Roger's cell phone. He reported that the civil suit trial was to start in two weeks, and he needed to have a meeting with Roger and Evvy to prepare their testimony. They set a date and went on to enjoy their evening of celebration.

The following week Evvy and Roger met with Rueben in Atlanta. It was a long meeting and the thrust of the suit was that the family had suffered irreparable harm due to the incompetence and callousness of the Sheriff's office and the office of the prosecutor. The suit alleged that Evvy, each of the children and Roger were each subjected to harassment, the destruction of personal property, and the scorn of the community. They were made to feel uncomfortable, and in several incidents their personal well being was threatened. Jackman asked Evvy and Roger if they were agreeable to suing for five hundred thousand in compensation. They thought it was a bit much but they said fine as Jackman deserved a good pay day out of all this. Jackman said he had a little surprise for Roger and Evvy, and he handed them a check for six thousand, eight hundred, seventy three dollars and thirty-seven cents from Homeowners Mutual Insurance Company. It covered four thousand dollars in compensatory damages and the balance for reimbursement of actual damages covering the house, Roger's tires, etc. Rueben asked if it was acceptable. Roger and Evvy agreed it was more than adequate, and that they would write a check to Rueben for his thirty percent. Rueben declined as he said all he did was write a three paragraph letter.

The trial went very well as Jackman presented a compelling case of prejudice, arrogance, indifference, and incompetence. Evvy and Roger testified to the humiliation, terrorizing their children, and damages to their property, and dangers to their person. The City of Greenville had virtually no defense and the Jury awarded the full five hundred thousand that Jackman had demanded. There was talk of an appeal, but saner heads prevailed on the city council and two months later Roger and Evvy received their check for five hundred thousand dollars. Roger sent a check to Jackman for one hundred and fifty thousand, his thirty percent fee.

CHAPTER 33

Roger and Evvy spent many hours talking about what they should do with this sudden windfall. They felt that they were entitled to every penny, but they wanted to do something constructive. The Greenville County Fair was to be held in ten days and Evvy and Roger decided what they wanted to do with the money. Roger requested five minutes as a speaker during the opening day ceremony. After the notoriety of the trial and the replacement of a number of members of the sheriff's office, the officials running the fair did not want to involve the county or themselves in any further controversy, as a result, they readily agreed that Roger and Evvy could have five minutes of speaking time.

The Fair opened on a Saturday morning so it was well attended. As Roger and Evvy sat on the speaker's platform they were surprised at the number of citizens attending the opening day ceremonies. It was a bright sunny day and after speeches by the Mayor of Greenville, the President of the County Council, and the Chairman of the Fair Commission, it was Roger's turn at the dais. Roger and Evvy stood together and Roger started.

"My fellow citizens, my wife, Evvy, and I are pleased to be here today, and have this opportunity to speak with you. As many of you know, my family and I have recently been involved in legal disputes with the local government and it's law enforcement agencies. We prevailed in our disputes and as a result we received a settlement of three hundred and fifty thousand dollars, after attorney fees. We puzzled what should we do with this windfall. Many purposes came to mind. With two children who are one day going to go to college we strongly considered putting it into safe investments. This made us think that there are many deserving African-American students who will never make it to college, because they lack the funding that a college education requires.

We thought our two children are very fortunate as both Evvy and I are college graduates and have very responsible, well paying jobs. We will have the ability to see to it that our kids will go to college. We will insist that they work part-time to support themselves as the work ethic is an important part of their education. Other children are not as fortunate; they come from one parent homes, where in most cases the fathers have not had the sense, decency, and compassion to take responsibility for their children's day to day needs, let alone their future. Others come from homes where education means the local schools are providing baby-sitting services. Many who are uneducated envy those who have succeeded through hard work and a solid education. My fellow citizens this is wrong, such people regardless of race should be held up as role models for our youth. Instead our culture seems to idolize the drug dealers and criminals who have attained their wealth illegally, and at the expense of society.

As a result of our concerns, Evvy and I are donating the full amount of our award to the local chapter of the United Negro College Fund. We feel that in a way this is giving the money back to the community. All of us must embrace education. Blacks and many poor whites in many areas of our nation are the downtrodden, the menial laborers who in many cases break their backs everyday for barely livable salaries. We, our society, then looks at the crime statistics and we fill our prisons with young black men, and we say blacks are untrustworthy, they commit crimes, mostly against fellow blacks, many are drug users, and addicts. Many shake their heads and say "See, we've got to keep them in their place, or they will destroy our way of life." With such prevailing attitudes they receive little or no respect. They are addressed as "Boy" or "Nigger" and constantly feel the threat of violence and arrest. The best they can do for employment is day laborers, janitors, sewage workers, etc., at wages that won't support one person let alone a family. There is nothing wrong with any honest labor as we must respect the person who works regardless of his or her status, and we must pay them a fair and livable wage.

If we want to break this cycle and give all of our citizens a future worth striving for, we must do everything we can to provide the best education possible for our youth. I hope that our donation will in a small way help to break this cycle of poverty and despair for at least some of our future citizens. The minimum wage must be increased in our community as well as across our great nation. To this end, Sperling Mattress Company has instituted a minimum starting wage of ten dollars per hour in our plants. In closing, I just want to say that Evvy and I hold no animosity to the people of this community. Our neighbors have been very supportive and where there could have been problems, we have felt acceptance and enjoyed your Southern Hospitality. Thank you and God Bless you and our great nation."

A loud cheer and applause arose from the crowd. The full text of Roger's speech was reprinted in the Greenville Sentinel. The barely existent Democratic party and the State

Republican party took notice and began courting Roger as his speech was favorably received by the citizens of the area. Roger made it quite clear to all, he had no interest in politics or any sort of public office. As Roger said, "My work at Sperling is not done and it never will be until I retire."

His efforts were ultimately successful in purchasing the Jacksonville plant, and he was now looking at a plant in Miami. With the new equipment labor cost declined while profits increased. Isaac Newfeld was very happy and he saw to it that Roger was well rewarded with huge annual bonuses for his efforts. In addition Sperling Mattress Company established The Sperling Foundation which awarded five fully paid scholarships each year to deserving students at the University of South Carolina.

Roger and Evvy became very involved with several local charities and cultural institutions, and they were applauded for their generosity and philanthropic efforts. The following year the Maynards were named family of the year in the Greenville area, a first for any black family. They had found the acceptance and Southern Hospitality which they sought so many months before during their crisis.

The End